Old Shorts and Poetree
Book One

To Gina
My favorite salesperson ever!
(Don't tell anyone I said that)

OLD SHORTS
and
POETREE
Book One

Ron Runeborg

Published 2014 by Cleftomania

Copyright © 2014 by Ron J. Runeborg

All rights reserved. This book or any portion thereof may not be reproduced or used in any manner whatsoever without the express written permission of the publisher except for the use of brief quotations in a book review or scholarly journal.

First Printing:2014

ISBN 978-1-312-33048-1

Published by Cleftomania
Lakeville Mn. 55044

For information contact

oldshorts@gmx.com

For Linda, who gives me reason

For Karen Conley who kept on pushin

For all the dear friends who demanded it could be done

And for Andrew; because it's my book……………………

and I can do whatever I want

A Book

It's of no consequence without your touch, your ear, your approval

It provides no comfort beyond what you can find in its honesty

if honesty is indeed what you seek

It requires participation
a willingness to see beyond the horizon, a desire to know the unknowable

a wont to suspend disbelief, if just for a moment

One moment is all it asks

Ron Runeborg

INTRODUCTION

This book is an anthology, a smattering, a hodgepodge, a text mélange of the stuff that wanders around in the dark recesses of my rather odd brain. It is, technically, filled with Short Stories (otherwise known as drabbles, flash fictions, anecdotes, clever repartees, tiny novels or Attention Deficit Disordered Readers' Delights~ADDRDs), and Poetry in all its many forms including "Verse", "Unverse", "Free Verse", "Moderately Expensive Verse" and "Pretty Gibberish".

Though you may think there is a lot of material within these covers, I could have made this tome large enough for your young children to use it as a stool with which they might steal handfuls of cookies from your then accessible jar; so consider yourself blessed by my thoughtful brevity.

I started the process of creating a table of contents once I'd completed this work. As it would have taken somewhere near 4 pages to document every title contained, I determined that the price of the book would rise astronomically due to the quantity of ink needed to make all those little dots one needs to make a line from name to page number, so while you may find not having reference to your favorite tale might be frustrating, think about all the money I saved you.
Were I not the author and instead a reader, I would see this work in this way. This is a book that would go perfectly on a nightstand, next to a calendar of devotions or happiness platitudes. This could be a thing you do just before you pass out from the rigors of your day to days; read one story, or one poem, and then, have happy dreams. Invest in a bookmark!

Acknowledgements

I want to thank Kurt Deunick, a fine friend and artist who imagined and created the cover art for both this book and "Songs of Bragi Stringbreaker, King's Bard", and the cartoon of yours truly below.

May Kurt and his lovely bride live long and prosper

Ron Runeborg

Preface

My mother, patron saint of the psychotic, would buy a new spiral notebook every week, sometimes more often yet. She kept it on the kitchen table, where she likely spent 70% of her life. It would sit next to the sugar bowl, salt and pepper, coffee cup rack, her cigarettes and the huge, glass ashtray.

She'd doodle...all day...all night. She solved her oral fixation with smokes, her "being wanted" fixation with talking on the phone for hours and yet she still had so much nervous energy that she had cheap, ballpoint pens in hand nearly 24/7.

Dinnertime? She's at the table. She sets down her smoke and picks up the pen. A few dozen artworks later she sets down the pen and picks up the smoke, moves to the stove and stirs something. Then sets down her smoke, picks up the pen and so on.

She was multitasking, a pioneer, a living testament to the fact that some people CAN walk and chew gum at the same time. Sometimes I'd find her smoking, talking on the phone, nibbling on licorice sticks, doodling and cooking, and then she'd add a conversation with her number one son. Maybe it took all that to keep her mind from wandering into places better left alone.

I wish I could say I have notebooks filled with cartoons or little artsy renditions of my siblings and myself. It'd be great if it was a collection of house plans or wilderness scenes. It's none of those things. Had I saved them they'd contain pages and pages and pages of......little triangles.

They'd touch each other, sometimes vertically, some horizontally. I'm sure a shrink would have some explanation for that, some deep meaning that eludes me. All I saw was triangles; rows and rows of 'em. Some would be colored in, some had little spirals inside. Sometimes they'd be inked over something she'd written; once in a while they'd be covering a voodoo doll with pins sticking out, but mostly, just triangles.

I should have bought stock in the notebook company. I don't remember her ever not doing it, so do the math; say 75 notebooks a year times the 34 plus years I was her son before she passed...that's 2550 books with an average of 100 pages. Think about how staggering that is...255000 pages of little triangles, some with spirals inside, some colored in, all touching. At likely six or seven hundred triangles per page.......gods my brain nearly explodes.

Everyone picks up some habit of their parents, it's inevitable, it rubs off. If you're lucky it's not belching in public for a laugh or buying closets full of wing tip shoes.

If a computer keyboard had a triangle key, maybe I'd be doing little triangles with stick figure people inside; my variation on the theme. But instead, I write poems and little stories, reams and reams of both. So what you're hearing from me isn't truly made of whole cloth; it's weaved of genetic material, the doodles of a doodling son trained subconsciously by a doodling mother. We should all be so lucky.

If only that key existed you could be staring at pages and pages of triangles rather than the babbling of a madman. I've never seen that key. Your loss.

Chat Room Log ("everybody into the shower...")

Routine director: Yes, showering is boring but it must be done; so let's get going before imagination stops everything in its tracks.
Masculinity: Crank dem nozzles, let make dis ting hot Hot HOT!!!
Feminine Side: Moderation please, our skin's so sensitive, I hate looking like a lobster. And then the scratching!
Practicality: More heat, more sweat, less soap needed, less unremovable scum, money saved...
Imagination: So are we all ready for a nice daydream?
Philosophy: Well, I was thinking a little ponderance would be fun.
Child: Sandbox, Sandbox, Sandbox, Sandbox
Lust: I have plenty of topics we could think about... Take breasts for example...
Morals: Shush, there's a child in here!
Ethics: It's really not a child; it's only a manifestation o.....
Annoyance: Gods but you two are boring! Morals and ethics are ***DEAD!*** Get with the program!
Paranoia: You don't think anyone can hear us do ya? What if we're really loud and someone....
Impatience: Ok.. enough already! Yo! Philosophy! Wh...
Philosophy: Call me Phil
Impatience: Ok, Phil then! What was your idea?
Philosophy: I was just thinking...as one does… How seriously should we take internet relationships?
Confusion: Explain please, I don't get it at all
Know it All: He means should we treat these paper people as if they're real people!

Philosophy: Well, that's not exactly what I th....
Know it All: Of course it is!
Aggravation: Damn, I hate know it alls! Shuttup and let Phil speak!
Profundity: I could say it more deeply I'm sure.
Simplicity: Yea, and then we'll all just stare at you and wonder what the hell's your problem!
Philosophy: I'll try to elaborate
Verbosity: Yay! Go You!!! Take your time, we've got all the words in the dictionary! Why I remember one time when I was asked to elaborate and it took near 25 pages to f...
Brevity: We Get the POINT!!!
Seritonin Uptake Inhibitor Now calm down Brev, he means no harm. There'll be no rage here, I don't want to have to increase the dosage!
Rage: I don't get to do crap anymore; you guys suck!
Serendipity: Let's have a picnic and talk about Rage's inability to get it up!
Diplomacy: Now people, Philosophy was first, let's be polite and take turns, there's plenty of shower time for all of us.
Grace Under Fire: Please Phil, won't you enlighten us?
Philosophy: Okies. Let's say we have a friend from the internet, and that person tends toward silence for all but a few weeks a year. Now let's say we really care about that person, and we think they really care about us...
Self doubt: Wait wait! What's our caring worth, anything? Or is it just empty rhetoric like most of what we spew…
Confidence: Actually our caring is worth quite a bit; in the scheme of things, when measured against the majority of humankind's caring, based on the d....
Reality: Please! Let's not get stupid here, caring is caring alright? There's no way to qualify a concept. Move on!

Philosophy: As I was saying... We think they really care about u...
Melancholy: Obviously your example is dead on arrival. Care about us? Are you nuts?
Depression: Nobody cares about us... And **I Mean IT!**
Suicidal Tendency: Hang on, let me get a rope; I wonder if this shower pipe will hold our fat ass…
Pride: Just because we're a bit overweight you don't have to get vulgar!
Cowardice: No! No! Don't kill us by hanging!! Isn't there a full bottle of Ibuprofen we could swallow or something like that? How about we just eat Oreos nonstop. That'll kill us eventually! Or tapioca! Maybe we could choke on a pearl!
Wishful Thinking: We were supposed to go on a diet last week. Wouldn't that have been great?
Disgust: Oh yea baby. Gimme that meat and cheese!
Regularity: Oh God not that again. Atkins is dead. Leave his diet die with him! Gimme roughage!
Imagination: And then I was flying a kite over the Amazon when an alligator jumped out of the forest canopy and bit onto the tail of torn sheets and shouted "Take me to Peru or this kite's goin down my friend!"
Innocence: Holy Shit, where did that come from!
Resignation: Get used to it kid, it's every freaking day like this. In, out, in, out, the guy never knows what he's sayin he just babbles off some story like his lips are a nail gun and he's building a house.
Whimsy: Geez, let him babble, what's the harm?
Routine Director: Shuttup everyone, I hear noise on the outside!
Paranoia: I knew it; someone heard us and called the nuthouse!

Ron? Ron? Phone call!

Reality: Oh great. Shower's over.
Sloth: I'm not movin, in fact I might just stand here all day.
Paranoia: It's some government therapist trying to commit us, I just know it is!
Greed: But it might be Ed McMahon with a check for a million dollars from Publisher's Clearing house!
Hope: It could be Oprah who's been turned onto the blog we write and has decided that we're the next great author she wants everyone in her book club to read!
Cynicism: Shuttup you moron!
Crabbiness: Yea shuttup!
Brutal Honesty: Oprah doesn't read blogs.
Curiosity: Really? How do you know?
Know it all: He just knows, so shuttup!
Aggravation: Damn, I hate know it alls!
Paranoia: You guys scare me!
Testosterone: I'm gonna scare you into next week if you don't stop whining!

Ron? Are you gonna take the call or what?

Imagination: And then I looked under the bed and you know what I saw? Yes yes, underwear, a half eaten apple, a book of funny hillbilly quotes, a dead moth, a Penthouse and... **A MONSTER!!!**

Coming dear!

Opportunism: Routine director, start dryin us off... Inspiration! Take notes! Imagination, What kinda monster exactly?

Ron Runeborg

Can't We All Just Get Along

Why are we alone daddy?

Well, we're not really, we have mommy, she's just out looking for food.

I meant all three of us. Why are we alone?

Because everyone else is dead Junior.

Why did they die daddy?

It's a long story Junior.

Do we have to be somewhere soon?

You have me there son. Ok, this is why. It started with the ordinary people. The farm workers and truck drivers and custodians and dock hands. The rich people got tired of them, always whining about never having enough, always committing physical crimes, always being unhappy and vulgar. So the rich people started wars, and they sent all the ordinary people off to other places to kill each other, until the wars were over, and then they just stopped paying attention to the survivors until one by one they died.

So how come there's no rich people?

Well, once the ordinary people were all dead the rich people discovered none of them had learned how to do all those mundane tasks the ordinary people did, so they went without cleaning crews and bakers and grocers and infrastructure maintenance folk and the world was over time smothered in rot and disease and starvation.

Couldn't the rich people make their own food?

Oh, some tried to eat the products of their own labors, but they found there was virtually zero nutritional quality in ledger sheets, whether by the individual page or by the entire vault full.

Was that the only food they could make?

Oh some could cook alright, there were a few of their women who were just bored enough to learn a toaster from an easy bake oven, but without the farm laborers and the butchers and the millers and even the people that operated the machinery to turn chicken beaks into pink slurry that could be molded into McNuggets, not to mention the power plant operators who would create the juice to run the microwaves that served as rich people ovens, they couldn't heat anything anyway, and once you are accustomed to a certain standard of living, so I hear, cold food just isn't worth eating unless it's smothered in caviar… and without fisherpeople… you see the problem son.

But…

That's enough son, your mom can explain more if you like, I'm tired of speaking about the past.

Just one last question daddy, one that's different from those others?

Sure kid, one more. Shoot.

Why are we still here daddy? Aren't you either an ordinary person or a rich person?

I am a warrior son; a mercenary. The rich people hired me to kill the ordinary people who were stealing their money, and the ordinary people hired me to kill the rich people who were stealing their lives. Once they were all dead, I only had to kill the other mercenaries, and lucky for your mommy and you, I'm very, very good at what I do.

Then King for Show, Now CEO
 Into the fray the hundred rode
the battle turned quite nicely.
The king announced from his commode
"My plan hath worked precisely!
I knew if I were occupied
my knights would take the lead.
As general I'm disqualified.
I do so hate to bleed!"

The Dreams of Paupers

He dreamed of blue unfettered skies, of deeply tilled black soil He heard his mother calling, his release from sweaty toil, and with his family, said a prayer of thanks for all they'd known; then feasted over laughter, of the crops they all had grown.

She dreamed of fear and darkness, of the shadow piercing eyes; of bullets, bombs and bayonets, of shocked and "awe-full" cries. Her brothers perished all around, her sisters dragged away; the smell of smoke, the taste of bile, the predator and prey.

He dreamed of buglers mournful notes, of biers and fresh dug holes. He witnessed dead men's eulogies, a credit to their roles. He saw the laughing reaper, how his succubi did dance. He heard the cries of boys and girls who never had a chance.

She dreamed of cabins in the woods, of fresh blackberry jam, of climbing stoic Castle Rock, of scrambled eggs and Spam. She held her dying father's hand and whispered there of peace; and she hugged her mother tightly wishing life might never cease

And then the watch was over and the "ass in gear" was howled. Communal morning pleasantries were less exchanged than growled. The soldiers rounded up their guns and took their final yawns; another day of madness for the paupers and the pawns.

Ron Runeborg

Daddy's Little White Contraception

"Daddy? What's contraceptive mean?"

Tad choked on his beer, and while he coughed himself back into breathing he thought very carefully. Is the kid the right age for this? Am I the guy who needs to explain all that? And if I do explain this, does that mean I'll have to do the whole damned talk right now? Crap! Where's his mother!

"Contraceptive?" he said. "Well that's a very complicated word, but if you really, really want, I'll tell you."

"Yes daddy, I really, really want," Bascomb said with a great big smile on his ten year old face.

"Ok son, well, you see, there was this terrible army down in a country down by Mexico. You know where Mexico is doncha champ?" Once the nod came he continued. "Well, these guys were really bad people, and they called themselves the Contras!"

"I think I get that part" said Basc, "but what does the erraaaceptive mean?"

"You know when someone's trying to fool you? Well, that's called being deceptive! And the Contras were always tryin to fool people into thinking they were the good guys and not the bad guys. So when people lie real bad, Americans call them Contraceptives!"

Bascomb thought about that for a few minutes, and then his eyes lit up, signaling his having connected with the explanation.

"Daddy" he asked, what's an Exile?"

"That's when a place used to be an island and then all the water dried up. Then it's an ex Isle. Geez kid, did your mom say how long she'd be?"

Gimme that Old Tyme Religion

As his sword slid into the tender back of a praying priest, Herbert stopped to ponder a moment, holding his now dead victim off the ground by the magic of impalement.

"But, these look like they're ours Mortimer; are we sure these are not the clergy of the Church of the Sacrosanct Bakery Goods?"

Mortimer slit the throat of a pleading altar boy before he answered.

"I'm afraid not Bert; these heathens pray to our god I hear, but they eat crackers in bed! By their very existence they blaspheme the Holy Sisters of the Spotless Linen!"

"Oh my goodness!" Herbert shouted above the screams of his next target. "They shall suffer at the tip of my sword for this heresy! *EAT THIS* he screamed, thrusting his weapon into another man of the cloth and driving him backward until he'd toppled into a chaise lounge smothered in cracker crumbs.

Ron Runeborg

The Frightful Competition

"What's wrong?" I whispered. "I never feel you around anymore."

"I've been here all along kid" he answered in that moany groany voice I'd always imagined. "But I don't have any impact on those that don't believe in me."

"I believe!" I protested. "I'm as scared as I always was!"

He was silent for a moment, as if he was pondering the depth of my honesty. "I know you are son, but now it's of reality, you see? You fear terrorism and anarchy, you think about black helicopters and government agents searching through your grade school science fair memorabilia. You are afraid that the air is giving you cancer, that the Chinese are planning to take over the world."

I laughed. "Are you trying to say I'm a nutcase?"

He laughed as well. "Nah, you're pretty normal, everyone has similar fears, only the names change."

"But" I said, "life was a lot more fun when I was afraid of you!"

"I'm very flattered lad, but boogeymen don't have much sway once a person reaches puberty; or at least by eighteen or so except in the most neurotic of you humans. Still, you *can* be afraid of me if you choose. It *would* be less complicated for you no doubt."

I thought about his logic. It was true really; being afraid of nothing was much easier than being afraid of something, and it satisfied the human impulse to fear the unknown.

"I never stopped being afraid of the boogeyman you know" I said with a slight quiver in my voice; "I was ju..."

The boogeyman flew from under the bed and grabbed my feet, clutching and pulling at me while I screamed and fought back until victorious.

"Thanks man" he whispered once we'd both caught our breath. "It was lonely under here without your faith."

I leaned over the side of the bed, lifted the covers off the floor and caught sight of his beady little red glowing eyes hidden deep within the darkness. "No; thank **you**!" I nearly shouted before I hushed myself. "That was great! I'd forgotten how fun that could be!"

"Come back real soon, wontcha?" he slurred as we both closed our eyes and settled in for a night's sleep.

"I promise" I said. "Next time I see an underpants bomber. Should be any day now!"

Velvet Chisel

Susan's anxiety was beginning to transform into tightened muscles and a light headache. She needed to make a decision or there wouldn't be enough time to create <u>any</u> memorial much less one perfectly designed.

Her father Jack was a kind man, a brilliant man. He'd always been there to support her, even in his worst days; even at the moment of his death he was caring only for her. They'd been through a lot together, but nothing more telling than the accidental death of her mother and two brothers in a horrible freeway crash. She'd crumbled. His pain was at least hers, and yet he held strong to lead her through hell and to a life of joy and purpose.

She'd considered hundreds of quotes that might speak for him, Thoreau, Frost, Whitman, Thomas Aquinas, Martin Luther; even speech from his favorite characters, fact and fiction, the likes of Doc Holliday and Jack Ryan, Jean-Luc Picard and Arthur Pendragon. But after a time it all ran together, each phrase important unto itself, linked to his life and parallel to his intellect, yet lacking in soul and devoid of her love's expression.

It was almost four o'clock; she had no more time to debate, the decision was about to be made for her by default. Susan slipped from her car and walked to the door of Barnard's Stone Company. The office was empty though she could hear sporadic noises coming from behind a steel door, and so she swung it open, hoping her appointment had not been forgotten and the man she was to meet would be inside.

It was the workshop she stepped into, a plain room of concrete and block, its walls covered in steel scaffolding on which was stored slabs of granite and marble, and stone of other textures and colors she didn't recognize. There was a shirtless man in the room's center, facing away from Susan at that moment, seated on a tiny stool and surrounded by tools of all shapes and sizes. She thought to say hello, though the man's dress, or undress as it were startled her a bit. Before she could speak her eyes began to absorb what lay before her.

It was a carver she supposed. She'd never seen it done but she could just see the headstone beyond the worker's massive shoulders, and she watched as his fingers stroked the stone as if it were fragile as spun glass. He reached to his right and retrieved a small rattail file from the mass of picks and prods by touch alone; his head rocked back slightly, twisting left and right as if he were listening to a choir. And then he leaned into the slab and gently worked the file into an unseen crevice, rasping once, then feeling his cut and pondering its imperfections.

Susan moved a few steps to her left, never taking her eyes off the artisan and his canvas. She lost all peripheral vision, so focused she was mesmerized by the unwitting performance. Now she could see his profile, and as he moved his head, she viewed his face. His eyes were white, he was blind yet he had full use of the environment within his reach. He seemed to know where each of his dozens of tools were laying, and used each with such precision and grace it appeared as if he were a surgeon operating on his own loved one.

The words were as simple as they get in the business of death,

"Rest In Peace" was all the stone spoke. But the three capitalized letters were done as in the Book of Kells, each blocked face housing a menagerie of birds and mice, clinging to vines and their trumpeting flowers.

She nearly fainted when she heard a voice at her back, yet still her eyes never moved.

"He's a marvel, miss; Jack's blind, near deaf and has an IQ no bigger than a breadbox, but he cuts stone as if it was butter. He makes marble sing."

"His name's Jack?" she whispered, barely able to speak at all.

"We call him Jack the Ripper, miss" the man chuckled; "but don't get the wrong idea. It's because the only words he can spell are Rest In Peace, so the only carving he does is this; R.I.P. Sorry ma'am, it's an in house joke; it's only meant to be funny. This is a somber business; our humor tends to be a bit off color."

Susan smiled. "It is a little" she said; "a little funny. He's such a gentle man, he works the stone as if it's flesh, so careful that he doesn't hurt it in some way."

"To him it may be ma'am" replied the mason, Tom Barnard. "When we have no work commissioned I give him scraps and broken pieces; he hordes them as if they were puppies."

The artist set his tool on the floor, in the exact position from which he'd plucked it. Then he felt his work, sliding his fingers through every cut, following the contours of each animal, each plant.

Susan noted his light shivering. "Is he crying?"

"He's mourning the soul who will lie under his work. He's honoring the stranger who allowed him to present this gift, he's saying goodbye, in case no one else does."

Susan turned to the shopkeeper and wiped her own tears from her cheeks as he did the same. "He's my son, miss" Tom said; "I've watched him for 20 years now and I still tear up."

"Rest In Peace is perfect" she replied, working a slight smile into her offering. "My father will be well blessed by a gift such as this."

The Golden Age of The Church of the Ugly Stick

It fascinated me, each of my mother's sisters' wedding books nearly identical, all bound in white leatherette, all in black and white and all composed at Holy Name Catholic Church. Of course, that was before the ugly stick reconstructions of the sixties and seventies when chapel sanctuaries teeming with alabaster niches sporting saintly statuary were replaced by flavorless God warehouses; huge brick gymnasiums ad nauseam, church designers then touted as efficiency/chic.

In each photo a sister stood "with groom" before Holy Name's ivory altar; its magnificence dressed in gold embossed lace and covered in assorted dogmatic trinketry.

Ron Runeborg

The Homerun King of Linden Hills

I was the biggest kid on the block; well, except for Mike and he was slow we thought, so even if he showed up nobody wanted to pick him. He was so mean it was said he'd buy bunnies, and at night, pour gasoline on them and let them run...and then shoot them with his bow and gasoline soaked tampax tipped, flaming arrows. No one ever actually saw him doing that if I recall, but who would want to?

Nobody messed with Mike because he was crazy and huge; nobody except for my friend Tommy Lee. He fought the monster one day and whooped his ass, but he suffered a bite to his ear that made it swell up like a water balloon. Even though Mike lost, his reputation was enhanced because he was now a *dirty* fighter, **and** the meanest guy we knew.

Baseball was the game of choice in our neighborhood. It was 1965, the Twins were in the World Series and a lot of them lived within blocks of us, so we saw them once in a while at supermarkets and restaurants. We traded bubble gum cards and played metal mechanical baseball games with tiny balls and little wooden bats on pegs. We talked baseball all day, every day; except when we were talking about breasts or cars or how mean Mike was.

We played ball wherever we could within walking distance; a grade school tar parking lot with yellow, painted base paths, where I'd launch pitched tennis balls over the 3 story roofs of houses across Sheridan Avenue, or an empty gravel lot surrounded by chain link fence screaming *Climb me! Bend me!*

But mostly, we played in Linden Hills park; a jewel of the city park system with enough space to accommodate every kid for miles around.

The older kids always got the park diamonds before we'd get there, or if we'd claimed one first, they'd just bully us off their turf anyway. So we'd play in a tiny corner of the park, a splintered Webber Juniper as the backstop and rutted dirt splotches separating the bases and pitcher's mound from the weedy grass.

It was there I first discovered my secret talent. I could hit any ball a mile or more, so hard and so high no human eye could keep track of its flight. I owned a 34 inch, black Louisville Slugger that was almost as long as some of my friends were tall. But I was already close to six foot by 13, and the bat was perfect for me.

Everyone hated when I came to bat, especially the outfielders who were always the least liked guys on each team. Kid baseball is just like the adult model, nobody comes for the exercise, everyone wants to be the hero; so the best players always chose the positions that would mean less work and more glory, and the geeks got the open spaces where shagging balls was far more likely than catching them.

And when I hit them, it was not likely, but inevitable. The outfielders would try to back up far enough, but no kid wants to be so far from the rest of the guys that they feel like they're all alone. It was good for me, because *that* was never far enough when I was at the plate. As I remember it in my entire juvenile career I never had a ball caught, and never had to stand on a base. That made me a sort of neighborhood legend, the guy that other kids would, while passing me on the street would whisper BOOM! and we'd share a laugh. I was happy, had some small importance, a trade I could show off. I could hit the cover off a baseball.

Then, as always in my life, everything went to hell. Mike decided he wanted to play baseball.

Things were fine at first, he was slow as I said we thought, and slow guys are klutzy. He struck out a lot and everyone stayed clear of him since he was the meanest guy we knew and he'd get pretty damn mad when he struck out. But eventually he began to find the spot and connect with every pitch, and he could hit the ball even farther than I could, though I'd never have admitted that at the time for obvious reasons. We started to argue about it, as rival "coaches" would pick their teams. Mike and I would be first to go on opposite sides and everyone would ooh and ahh and swear their team was gonna win because of the power of their personal ape.

He'd hit a home run and his teammates would shout that it was the furthest ever hit, and then I'd hit one and my team would nya nya our opponents. It got pretty nasty at times unless Mike made his trademark mean face and scared the beejeebers out of everyone. So I suppose it was fate that we'd eventually have a homerun contest in which only Mike and I would face off to see who was **really** the homerun king once and for all.

Well the day came and it was bright and sunny as was every day I can remember of my youth. Every kid from the neighborhood was there and even a few of the older kids showed up, but mostly to razz us and to taunt Mike because they thought he was slow. But me and the guys stuck up for Mike cuz he was one of our own and even though we thought he was slow and damned mean, we couldn't let an older kid make us look bad. So we chased them off with baseball bats; kind of an homage' to Mike's meanness.

Then it was batting time and Mike hit a few and I hit a few, each landing marked with a flat rock or crushed soda can or some piece of garbage pulled from the park board clubhouse cans before the event. We were neck and neck for a while when Mike began to really wallop his pitches and his hamburger wrappers and dirt clods were moving further and further away from mine.

I was watching my fifteen minutes of fame vanish; though in reality it hadn't been invented yet. If I lost, I'd be thrust back into sullen anonymity; instead of calling me Ron as they had all summer, I'd be back to running board or runaround or some other humiliating derivative of my surname. I'd once again be a nobody, and I was just getting used to being a somebody.

So it's no surprise that on my turn I was putting everything I had into whacking the balls as far as I was able. I wasn't quite as large as the meanest guy in the neighborhood, but I had rhythm, and my slightly smaller biceps could dance; especially as compared to those of a slow guy.

On the last hit of the day, the pitcher offered me a gift like no other; slightly away, nice and low, a ball I could scoop up and send to heaven as only the real Linden Hills homerun king could. My stance was already closed and leaning back, and yet I had all the time in the world to lean further and pull my leg in one more notch as if a pitcher in a windup.

As I released I visualized Harmon Killebrew, the first basemen for the Twins and its own homerun king. Every molecule of my hundred seventy pound frame was concentrated on that black stick as it found its arc and followed the invisible yellow brick road to its intended target. My left leg raised and pushed out three feet if an inch, my shoulders widened, my back flexed and my wrists tugged as if I was pulling a jet plane across a bridge with lasso.

The thud was otherworldly, like a pumpkin dropped from a ten story building. The ball had not yet arrived and I'd connected with something malleable, something that slowed my forward progress, yet could not have stopped it dead if it had been a concrete post.

I can barely see the next few seconds as it was so unreal I'm sure my memory banks tucked it deep away within moments of its cranial inscription. A kid, perhaps five or six years old, had been sitting behind the catcher taunting me with the standard "swing batter batter"; a kid related to Mike, a cousin in town and dragged to the contest by an unwilling Mike, forced by his mother to baby sit. A kid who was actually slower than slow as he'd suffered water on the brain when born, and was a little flighty and funny looking to a pack of 13 year old boys; perfect for teasing relentlessly had not his cousin and protector been Mike who would surely beat us all bloody had we said one unkind word.

The kid had spotted something across the park, some shiny bauble or kite in a tree, maybe even some imaginary monster that he wanted to meet firsthand. And so he took off after it without a care in the world, right across home plate.

The bat caught him right at the base of the skull and while I can't truly estimate how far I threw him, I can say with certainty he left the ground and his landed prone body was at least a few feet from the end of my Slugger in the end.

The world stopped its rotation to see what had happened. The kid wasn't breathing, Oh God! he wasn't breathing! There was no blood, but he was face down in the dirt, absolutely still.

The bat simply slipped from my fingers as I just stood there, paralyzed and trying to catch my own breath. I'd killed a kid, the ultimate crime against both God and man. I'd surely go to jail, and sooner or later to hell. I bled out every lousy rotten circumstance my miserable life had ever maliciously served up, watching the vulgarities of the few years I'd been alive flip across my mind's eye like oversized baseball cards in the spokes of a bicycle.

I can't tell you how it was that I didn't actually sever the child's head from his shoulders. I hit him with more power than a speeding car, in exactly the spot that should have popped his top into outer space.

But after a couple eternities, the kid sucked in a huge breath and started to cry; standing as he rubbed the back of his head and then running off in the direction of the shiny thing that started the whole affair.

I said nothing, but bent to pick up my black bat, turned toward home and started walking, alone, in total silence.

I heard plenty of "Holy shit did you see that!?"s until I was out of earshot, but no one ran to my side to offer me a "wasn't your fault" or the like. My career was over, the homerun king was dead.

I didn't play baseball the rest of that summer, I turned to playing music badly, though on multiple instruments, to chatting with albino squirrels and to sitting alone on a flat roof three stories above the planet's crust, peering through the darkness as if I were Batman watching over Gotham in the gloom.

I never played well again, always looking over my shoulder, forever nervous at the plate that giving it all I had might result in an accident from which someone might never recover; someone much younger than I who might better progress through life without my interference in the form of a black Louisville Slugger to the back of the skull.

But for a while I was somebody; I was the Homerun King of Linden Hills for one whole summer. It was great to be royalty for even a single tick of the clock of the Milky Way, and an eternal blessing that I didn't walk from that field the killer of a tiny, quite slow child I'd never seen before, nor since. I only hope his life was one filled with chasing baubles. He and I would have that in common.

Little Dog Agog

From deep within the black furball that rests on my unmade bed I see the stark white iris of a single eyeball, rotating in time with my movements. He is still entranced by the sandman's song, yet the excitement of knowing what is about to happen forces one lid to the upright and locked position lest he miss his witness of the supernatural. A second eye opens as I undress. (I feel it more than see it as I must concentrate on relieving myself of my jockeys without distraction or meet the floor face to face)

As I move toward the master bath I hear the telltale tinkle of a nametag and license. His head had surely risen. He is aware. He is coming. And yet there is no movement below the shoulders until the sound made as I slide the shower door back and reach into the stall to grip the controls.

Suddenly there is a flurry of activity. The bed and the little dog part company as if one is a cannon and the other, an unemployed college student unable to find any job save this one left in the circus. His face, cute even while disheveled, appears in the doorway and the stare down begins. He waits, patiently, his tail moving in a circular motion signifying great anticipation. I can taunt him no more. I pull the knob thingy and water gushes forth; from high up on the wall, from where there **had been no water moments before**.

He stands like an ebon statuary, eyes pinned to the gush, head cocked ever so slightly; and then without fanfare he turns to go, acting as if he'd lost interest in the blink of that singular white iris buried within a mass of curly black fur. Another day has come. Another miracle has transpired. It's time for a nap.

Ron Runeborg

Perennial Pook

I once lived alone in a house that backed up to a big woods. I worked overnights at the time, finding my way home at just about dawn in the spring and summer; and waiting for me each morning was a neighborhood mutt I called "Pookie" or, more often just Pook. She was a flop eared thing, maybe Springer and Sheltie I'd guessed, but whatever her genes, her time was rapidly running out.

I always had some surprise treat for her so Pook would race me to my driveway; her aged legs barely able to carry her anemic weight, she more dragged herself to my side and then lay down to catch her breath as I gave her some lovin' till she was ready to eat snacks.

I'd go on about her, but it was really an unremarkable relationship we had; just a man living alone and a smelly, unkempt feral mutt whose owner had likely tossed her out as she reached the decrepit stage of her life.

She and I would walk in the slow moving sunrise, down a trail we'd blazed through the miniature forest out my back door. Some days she'd lead me, others she followed so closely I had to take care not to pin her ears to the ground with my oversize boots; but every walk stopped at a fallen oak, its rotting carcass a fine bench for me, and an overhang shelter for Pookie. She had over time dug herself a nice shallow pit just under the log, shaded and cool and a perfect place to escape the sometimes overbearing heat of a Minnesota summer.

Then one morn she stopped showing up in my drive, and for a few days I just passed it off as circumstance. Maybe someone had taken her in, or worse, maybe the pound had snatched her. After three days I started to wonder, I kinda missed the little thing's visits...so I decided to look for her around the neighborhood.

Well into the afternoon I combed the streets and alleys within a mile of my house, asking anyone I passed if they'd seen her lately. My mention always forced a smile, everyone I spoke to knew her and thought she was the coolest mutt, but no one had seen her around.

Why it never occurred to me before that moment I don't know, but I suddenly thought to walk our trail in search. And sure enough, she'd been waiting for me all along. She'd curled up in her hidey-hole to draw her last breath, obviously having known that her time had come and making haste to be sure her final stop was at the log where we'd rest and munch on sweets and fake bacon strips. I admire that in Pook, and in dogs in general. They seem to know when the other side is knocking and normally pick some remembered, important spot they'd choose to spend eternity rather than simply running till they drop.

I've been daydreaming lately about traveling alone, seeing my image riding across mountain meadows and through miles of winter wheat. My visage is devoid of facial movement, only my eyes roam, drawing in every speck of color within my reach. I hear nothing and feel less; sight is my one sense and I am seemingly driven to see all that I can as quickly as possible.

I've had this urge before, and I've done a similar trip in my recent past, but this seems different somehow; as if there's some reason I don't yet understand. I've been in nearly every state in the continental US and I have no one that I'd care to visit as I did when I last hit the road alone, so I can't really imagine why I'd suffer the weather for a 5000 mile run around the block. Maybe it's just some wanderlust thing; watching the summer wane, pushing my dreams into overdrive.

I'm not putting the two stories together intentionally, but one had reminded me of the other and while I get the metaphor, I don't really believe the intimation at this point. No doubt it's just coincidence. In the meantime, I'd better get a tune up and new rubber; I may be goin for a ride.

Oh, and Pook? I buried the lass where she lay after using a steel rod and stone fulcrum to move the log far enough to have shovel space, and then rolling it back once she'd been protected from scavengers under a foot of soil. I don't pass that way very often anymore, but the once or twice a year I do, I still call to her and flash her a smile. I imagine I'm alone in my recall, but she was worth at least a memory and a few paragraphs written in space.

Into the Breach

I checked the mirror. I would definitely have to lose the Bermuda shorts and flip flops, but I wondered if I had the right outfit and accessories for this gang soirée or if I'd have to destroy some work clothing to get the job done.

As luck would have it, my two week old jeans were right where I'd dropped them, half standing of their own volition against the west bedroom wall. I could have gone with the shirtless look, all the thugs were doing it, just skin and jacket and call it good; but I decided I might need bandage material and rather than wearing a corpsman tool belt with assorted gauzes and tape, I selected a clean t-shirt that could be ripped into squares if necessary.

Then the sleeveless Levi colors, the low top cowboy hat complete with doggie choke chain and authentic squirrel tail, the pointy toed shitkickers, the fingerless black leather gloves, the skull rings, Harley primary chain belt, Vietnamese tasseled armband and spurs.

Finally I slipped my one and a half inch open end wrench into my belt, my stiletto into my custom boot compartment and a nine ounce sap into my jacket wine pocket.

I took one last look. I was hoping to intimidate a few adversaries into finding another target. If I were many of them, I'd back off from what faced me in the glass. Gang wars though were such a crap shoot. Sure as hell I'd show up dressed for bear and they'd show up with an elephant gun.

Ron Runeborg

The Pitch Black Room

It was two AM; it seemed like it was always two AM during those years I owned a recording studio. I always had far too much work for money, and the daytime was reserved for the non paying customers, musicians trying to hit the jackpot. So overnights were all I had left to cover the expense of my partner's dreams; that we'd one day break a record contract with one of his apprentices and all my labors recording and mixing industrial media would have been worth it.

The building had been a small hardware store originally; its only windows, street side. We'd bought it as a media co-op, me, a director, a couple photographers, programmers and two writers. My part of the space was far from daylight, a 20 yard walk from the front door down a long, narrow hallway. I'd taken two rooms, the first being a warehouse area all the way to the rear. It was perfect in size and shape and cinderblock construction to boot, but with linoleum tile floor and block walls, it was too "alive" in its raw state; so my partner and I covered the walls in insulation and cheap fabrics, and built a few sound reflectors to act as movable walls when needed.

The control room had been an office, a bit too small for equipment and clientele as is; so we kicked out a wall and expanded forward into the studio room, containing the door to the basement stair in the process. I had this grand idea that the window between one space and the other should be the size of a house. (Perhaps it was a testosterone thing.) The glass was four feet tall by eight feet wide in the end; great for seeing all the action during sessions, but a giant black hole when the studio itself was unlit.

And now it was two AM, and the black hole was as pitch. I may have mentioned my fear of the dark, a transient thing that I sometimes need to simply grit my teeth and control in order to get anything accomplished in my life. One overnight gig in the studio would be fine; the next, done with sweaty palms. I just forced myself to deal with it as I could hardly tell a client "Hey sorry, I missed your deadline but it was dark and I was afraid of monsters; I'm sure you understand."

The control room was done in dark earth tones, the lighting, moody if not downright unusable. The equipment itself was black and then there was the window. It's interesting what the subconscious does with peripheral images...as example, how would it know the reflection on black glass that keeps moving around in the edge of my vision is actually me, and not some demon behind the glass doing some voodoo dance to attract my attention, to be followed by his head peeling back and showing his bare skull or some such once I'd looked up?

Like I said, it was rare it even occurred to me there might be a demon behind the glass so it was no big deal. But this night, this night started at 2 AM and didn't end for quite some time.

I was fond of loud, so it was my procedure to have my mixing board cranked up all the time, feeding maximum signal to a few thousand watts of clean power and then into these massive speakers we'd had custom built into the walls.

It was an industrial soundtrack mix I'd come in for, a voiceover describing how "random company X" was nearly Godlike in all ways, accompanied by appropriately thumpy, horn blasting, hip classical, movie music and sound effects...my particular specialty.

The voiceover had been done by a local legend, Tom Barnard. You've heard him, no matter where you live. For years he flew to both coasts recording movie previews and McDonalds' spots; one year was the voice on seven of the fourteen major sponsors commercials during the Olympics, a feat that made him rich enough to stop commuting altogether. Let's say his voice is that of God, with throat cancer; deep as the grand canyon, raspy as a cheap steel file.

I'd recorded him during the afternoon, and now had to edit. Understand, this was 1979; recording was done on tape, editing done with a wax pencil to make the spot, and a razor blade to zip out the offending portion. It was tedious, but I was a master so it went pretty fast.

So as I walked into the studio at 2 AM, just that tiny bit on edge as I sometimes am at first when walking into a cavern without bright lights or windows to the real world. I swept through my beginning routines without even taking my coat off. Master power on, tape reel spun into place and leadered, editing block and tape moved into place and tape deck started. I would listen to a few paragraphs to put me in that special place between art and crass commercialism, where my best work was done. It was sort of my standard flourish I guess, a middle finger tossed off to my fears, ignoring the tingling in my spine and shouting "AHA" like a Monty Python character might to a Frenchman.

One last note, I'd been working on a job that afternoon that had required me to lower the tape speed as on that project quality was far less an issue than expense. I did it so rarely that it's no wonder I didn't remember.

As I slipped off my coat, my back to the black hole, the voice began. Imagine the deepest voice you've ever heard, in slow motion, half time actually. Now play it at 120 decibels, about the volume of a jet passing overhead so close you can jump up and tap the fuselage.

There's this feeling I get that maybe everyone else experiences in exactly the same way and we've just never told each other. It's pretty similar to that moment when I've tried to change a light fixture without flipping off the breaker because the basement's just too far away; and I touch two wired together. It's that jolt of electricity after which you quickly check yourself to make sure you're not smoking from any orifice.

I can't say for certain that in the split second decision to whip around and hit any switch that would end the terror, was a voice that said "remember, the black hole is that way too"; but I'm betting it was there. I *did* hit the switch, the voice *did* stop, and my mind's eye *did* catch the (perhaps) reflected movement slightly stage left (maybe it was a monster), and I suffered the same shock again only this time it nearly sat me down as my legs couldn't take the banging together.

It might have been a half hour before I regained my composure. Of course I wanted to turn on more lights, but the studio lights were actually out of the control room, down a little hall and then reach your hand into the pitch dark of a room so large any number of miscreant malevolencies could have been lurking; so I put that on hold for the time being.

It's always been a bit of a contest anyway, a sort of "you're too damn old for this fetish so open that door and fling yourself into the dungeon because if you don't I will shame you forever and ever." Otherwise I'd simply acknowledge I have this childish perhaps, but nevertheless <u>real</u> neurosis, and always turn the freaking lights on when I enter a room just in case; shame be damned.

Well, too late now, did I mention it was 2 AM? Just about then I start smelling this odd smell, though it was hard to tell through the cigarette smoke I'd just chained into existence. It was a little rotten eggy or I'd not have paid it any attention at all, but that being the nasal color of natural gas, I thought I should at least follow it a moment. Wouldn't ya know it, it led to the basement door; a basement that had a light switch certainly, but one I'd need to open the door to reach and it was about that time I noticed that it wasn't really eggy at all, but sulphuric, as if someone had been lighting match books because they'd been walled into the basement like some Amontillado thing and all they had to keep them warm was a stack of matchbooks with that draw Winky contest printed on them. Or maybe it was a gate to hell that just opened at the foot of the stairs; I couldn't decide without opening the door to take a look and if it *was* Asmodeus... that would have *really* spooked me. *No Kiddin!*

Well that kinda did it; I was really unnerved now and walked back to behind my desk doing my best to not catch my reflection in the window. I stood there wondering what to do, as my deadline wouldn't wait, but my heart pounding in my throat was making it tough to breathe and I was a little worried about being found face up, eyes wide in the morning; just one more young heart attack victim to add to Journal of Medicine statistics.

I stood there, torn between business reality and my reality, as fantasy as it is. And then something really strange happened.

From the pitch black studio room came a sound like no other.

Let's say you find this cymbal and next to it is a hammer and a little sign says "*break the cymbal, win a prize.*" So you grab the hammer and you lift it behind you, rock back on your feet and with every muscle in your body you steer that hammer into its upward arc, then drive down on the handle until contact with the thin metal of the noisemaker is complete.

And it rings and it rings and it rings and it rings......

I didn't know I could scream; well in fact, I couldn't. I *did* scream but all that came out was this weird airy sound, like emphysema patients wheeze when they sleep. I had to look of course, directly into the pitch black window, directly into my reflected face, its jaw open, eyes half shut, skin stretched taut, funny noise emanating, vision. I screamed a few times I'm sure, not that it helped much. I lost my footing and was now seated, my joints locked in place, my head pounding so hard I was sure there was a crowd inside my skull banging on the exit doors trying to escape the inferno within.

Yea sure, I rationalized. We'd been in the process of moving, stuff was boxed and stacked and otherwise strewn about. Maybe a cymbal had been set in an uncomfortable place and just decided that at 2 AM it would jump from wherever it was and hit the floor, standing on its side so that its little rivets could vibrate a half hour or two; a Zildjian perpetual motion machine.

Maybe it just wanted to crash one last time before we left the building; *Should auld acquaintance be forgot....*

After another 20 minutes or so I admitted the obvious. There was no way I'd be finishing that mix that night. It was time to go. The trouble was that I had to walk toward the pitch black room wherein the cymbal lie at rest (for the moment), the door swung wide open, leaking its pitch blackness into the hallway, just to get to the alarm system in a tiny closet across from that very room that I'd need to turn my back on.

Another ten minutes maybe and I'd worked up the courage to just do it, to walk the few feet and turn the key, and then turn, back to the pitch black room, and walk down the quarter block long, dimly lit narrow hallway with its 18 foot ceilings making it all too much like a "Looking Glass" experience.

I don't do horror flicks often, for obvious reasons; but I can't always ignore their promos which have in some cases been the grist of nightmares for years thereafter. Well at the time there were a few that showed either beings or objects flying down long, poorly lit, high ceilinged corridors in search of the next living thing to snatch, knock to the floor and drag screaming back into pitch black rooms with waiting cymbals and God knows what else. (Cue Toccata and Fugue in Dm)

Every step was an eternity, a constant fight with myself to not break into a run and destroy any droplet of personal pride left to me. I thought about just walking backward, but of course, "behind me" is relative; no matter how I did it, there would always be a "behind me."

Obviously I made it outside and to the safety of 3 AM streets in a college neighborhood of a large city, and for the next few minutes I stared at the glass door I'd just locked and visualized all manner of beast slam up against it from the inside, all foiled by my clever and hurried escape. I didn't really see anything and yes, I knew that, (like I've said I'm not actually crazy, just...odd) but my imagination played the grisly scene over and over as if it were trying to vent the fear that had built up for an hour, by spinning supernatural sights until the venom had all been spent.

I spent the night in a diner, well lit, plenty of company and coffee. I didn't go home until day had sprung, and I slept on the couch just to confuse the spooks in case they'd followed me home and hidden in my bedroom closet. I couldn't sleep long as I did have that deadline, and when I got back to work, I *did* find a cymbal lying on the floor; though how it got there I couldn't explain for the life of me.

It's all 30 years behind me now, we moved from that building soon after and I hadn't even thought about that night until writing this tale one dark and stormy you know what. I do once in a great while pass through that neighborhood, and I just can't resist driving by our old building; at this writing a mom and pop candy factory. But when I pass it at night, I rarely take the dare and actually stare into the pitch black, glass door as I pass; perhaps afraid that whatever chased me that night is still inside, and my urge to drive by is no urge at all, but a response to a calling.

Well, not really; but it sounds great in print.

Ron Runeborg

The End of the War of Words

I ducked as an idiom went whizzing past my head, so close it made me deaf in one ear and slightly off balance. Quickly I tossed off a short flurry of past participles and a nouned verb for good measure. He'd parried the PPs but the verbish caught him full on in the chest, and as he scrambled backward I added a morpheme and a pair of terms back to back, one of which glanced off his cheek setting him on "stagger".

I needed to go for the kill, I could hardly lift my banter by that point. I cut his legs out from under him with a scuttlebutt and the moment he hit the ground I raised two hoary conjunctives well over my head.

"Do you yield" I shrieked!

"Nevah" he said, spewing a cartoonish affectation which nearly brought me to my knees.

I drove my Hence and Therefore deep into his sentence, splaying his grammar, causing his vitriol to scatter. As he took his last breath I looked for and discovered a concordance with which I wiped his upchucked affectation off my breastplate, and then sat down to compose a set of bibliographical references that upon my triumphant return home I might enter the holy lexicon with glossary in hand.

Preface

It was cold; cold and damp and dark and Nebraska-ish. I'd been riding for hours, trying to get out in front of master winter who was desperately trying to stay relevant well into the first weeks of April. I was tired and cranky and chilled to the bone; my ass hurt, fingers ached and my desire to put as much distance between me and Minnesota was slowly being eroded by my need for a nicotine and sugar transfusion. Yet on the prairie, one roadside pullout looked the same as any other; grassy, treeless, lifeless, McDonalds wrapper strewn… I needed to stop but I refused to do so until I was beckoned by the unusual, or interesting, or at least trashless.

Then I saw a sign showing a bridgelike cartoon and a stick figure being tossed from it into the apparent water by forces unseen. "Warning" it said; "High wind area! Caution!" As my middle name as interpreted by ancient Celtic seers means "One who throws caution to the wind", I could think of no more perfect place to pull aside and demonstrate my power over nature by lighting a cigarette within a dangerous gale.

Sadly, the wind was on holiday at the fore end of the bridge. I sat upon a WPA concrete park bench, toking and Coke-ing and dreaming of those who might have sat in this place in days long past, which is what I generally did when solving all the world's problems in my head seemed like too much work.

It was a giant swamp before me, a fen perhaps, or slough. I saw no river nearby so I assumed it was just the crest of the local aquifer poking its head out of the limestone to be warmed by the sun. It was grassland, tall, waving in the breeze, green as a Leprechaun's breeches. Unlike the last 200 miles the land had a slight undulation to it, as if its maker had rolled out the dirt carpet but had forgotten to tamp it down. And then I saw them; the faces, the bones, the dust. I imagined a full story as I sat there, a re-creation of generic events, a telling of short, hard lives, of desperate struggle, of burgeoning hope, of man's inhumanity. I saw the blood pooling in the shallows, pulled out by the wind and set to a heartbeat metronome by white cap breakers crossing the breadth of the ancient pond.

I'd have cried had I had it in me, but cola makes lousy tears and hypothermia tends to stiffen manly resolve. Still, I said in whisper what I felt; that I knew it was all in my imagination, that it's as likely nothing happened here as not, and yet if something did I was tossing my empathy into the waters, my spirit, my warmth.

I had a second smoke and thought about the dichotomy of cruelty and beauty and of my species' relentless desire to comingle the two. But soon enough it was over and all I could think of was my stick figure self being tossed from a bridge in the middle of nowhere, to drown in solitary silence, to be retaken by the dust that made me what I am. I mounted and headed off toward Colorado Springs for another night and another hot shower in another motel; but not before promising to write down that story one day.

Sadly it took over a decade, and only by being prompted by a photograph did I remember my oath to the wind. It may or may not have been worth the effort, but I'm happy that for once I've actually fulfilled a pledge; even if it was only between me and , well, no one really…

Bones Untangled

There is a story I might tell, a yarn perhaps, a legend some say. It is about the day two became one and how the heat of burning truth set a field ablaze from that day forward.

In the spring of 1868, Henry Flockheart, his wife Amanda, son Christopher and daughter Brie were busy in their homestead's fields, tearing at the northern Nebraska sod so as to make furrows in which to plant a saleable crop of corn. Proud they'd survived the harsh winter and re-energized by longer days and warmer nights, the family bent to their task with a cheerful determination rarely seen in the faces of true pioneers.

A year earlier Henry had been an importer; a Bostonian businessman, fairly well-heeled and quite comfortable within his particular layer of New England's social strata. Then he'd discovered his partner had embezzled the entirety of the company's wealth and had vanished into the jungles of South America. An honorable man, Henry sold everything he owned in order to satisfy his debts, right down to his bifocals and straight razor. It was only happenstance that he should spot a notice printed above the fold of the Boston Globe, a newspaper he'd never bothered to read before this. As he was passing a newsstand located on Drake Street, the day's paper seemed to call out its header. "Unlucky Breaks? Need a New Start? Land for the asking!"

It had been Brie's dream originally, to live deep within the country, or the Wild West she'd read about. She loved the outdoors, had learned what a child could of the science of plant biology and propagation procedures and before she'd reached the age of 13 she'd created a middling forest of terra cotta potted plants in the Flockheart den.

Mrs. Flockheart was a librarian, and at the request of her husband had gathered a mountain of books written on agriculture, wilderness survival and home construction; all skills the family would need if they were to attempt a complete change of direction. Henry and Amanda had met while racing sailboats off the shoals of Nantucket Island, adventure was in their blood; and while they'd not have wished themselves into their predicament, it seemed almost a sign from God that they should tear free of the past and create a new legacy. Their children would learn the value of keeping an open and powerful imagination, the skill of seeing opportunity in even those things that seem impossible.

In the beginning, the group was daily fighting off the curse of discouragement. Growing accustomed to transportation by covered wagon and practicing the care and feeding of livestock were easy enough cultural adjustments. Going days without bathing in the dust and scorch, fending off black flies and mosquitoes, laboring through sickness and oppressive weather and rationing foodstuffs and drinking water on the other hand made their march westward seem a fool's errand.

But all that was behind them now. They'd suffered the trek, claimed their parcel and had arrived well before winter. The land they'd been granted was barren in part, save the tall foxtail and sedge of the Nebraska plains. But one boundary of their hundred acres was marked by the river Brule, and within the shadow of its flow grew hundreds of elm and oak, poplar and buckeye. And so with plenty of building material at hand, the house was begun and one room made weather tight before the snows and westerly winds howled out of the Rocky Mountains and buried the central grasslands.

A long day was spent by all four Flockhearts that late April. The earth was still veined with thin layers of ice just below the surface. It was early yet but only by a few days. Henry thought the weather too spectacular to miss a chance to plant slightly ahead of schedule, to not risk being rained out of the fields on the day when a book said it was "the right moment".

As the family gathered at the crest of a small hill between four fields and turned to walk home while arm in arm, they said a prayer of thanks, grateful that they'd been blessed with another chance at success.

An arrow through Henry's throat stopped the prayer before it had been finished. The group had no weapons. At the age of 11, Christopher had barely begun learning about the art of fisticuffs. Though Amanda had absorbed a great deal of the printed information she'd pulled together dealing with survival and defense, the sight of her husband dropping to the ground, his life's blood showering their two children, his eyes wide and vacant, made her forget every word she'd read. The mother rushed her attackers, screaming sailor's curse, and was wrestled to the ground by three Sioux men who had now dismounted and moved toward the group.

All three were dragged downhill to the edge of a swamp where atrocities were committed too foul to recount here. Their bodies and Henry's as well, were mutilated beyond recognition and left in the shallow waters to rot along with the vegetation.

In the summer of 1872, a Lakota warrior named Redhawk stopped alongside a small Nebraska watershed, giving his wife Migizi, his son Hek-ta-ena and his daughter Silver Feather a chance to dismount and rest near the cool, stagnant pool. It had been a good day. He'd seen no soldiers in nearly a week's time, the mountains he longed for were only another week north of sunset. It would be good to be home in the sacred Black Hills. It would be safe there, he could stop running and his family could exist in a shallow peace.

Surely it would only be a matter of time before the whites covered the dark green hills, infecting every inch of land between the two great mountain ranges. The Lakota were already being slaughtered, and those who were captured or had surrendered were being shipped to small parcels of worthless ground, to be fenced like cattle, left to starve, left to bleed out broken hearts.

But for this moment, Redhawk was free and would do as he pleased. His children would be fed, his woman would be warmed and his spirit would fly as foretold in his naming. All this would be true so long as he had one breath left within his chest. The clan of Redhawk would never be slaves to white man's greed.

He never heard the shot that killed him; the rifle was too powerful, the aim too true, the sniper too far off. Within the hour the mate and offspring of the great Lakota Redhawk were captured and killed, their mangled, bloodied bodies tossed into the pond; where they'd stopped to simply catch their breath in the midst of a long journey.

When the Redhawk clan and the Flockhearts met above the brackish waters, their bones entangled, their souls adrift, no words were needed to understand that they were kindred. They were two families, men brave and generous, women dedicated and strong, children honest and respectful. They were free spirits, in search of simple lives, hoping to be left in peace and offering the same in return. They were wary, but harbored no hatred; they wanted little, took less and gave back more. And yet through the ignorance of their fellow animals, they were executed for no more a crime than existence.

They understood that it was neither the white or red man to blame for their demise, but the fool; that the shadow of man's inhumanity darkened all nationalities, all races, all genders. And they knew that there is no more unbelievable sorrow, than is seen in the blood of children being shed without remorse, always without reason, forever without conscience.

It is said that the waters of a certain small Nebraska wetland run red in the spring and summer, that the blood of the world's innocent children rises through the stems of cattail and rush, sage and scrub, trying to escape the liquid grave in which it was poured; trying to rise above the evil that conspires to extinguish the very soul of mankind. It's rumored that the wind whispers through the grass and seed fluff of Flockheart swamp, and if one listens very closely, one will hear voices speaking in both English and Lakota. "May the fire burn bright until every man understands the horror. May we live to see the day that the well runs dry."

Ron Runeborg

The Jack and Jill Chronicles
"Another Fine Light Bulb"

Jack and Jill
went up the hill
to fetch a pail of water

Jack, the most industrious of Hilltown's young Republicans and a budding entrepreneur was deep in thought when Jill, his live in girlfriend and Hilltown's "Queen of the Riverboat Whistle Maidens", nearly ran him over.

"Geez Jill" he said, adding "you klutz" under his breath, "don't follow so close will ya? How many times have we come up here, and how many times have you damn near run me over?"

"I can't help it Jack" she said; "watchin the backs of your feet kinda hypnotizes me! How come I can never go up first and you follow me?"

"We tried that, remember? I can't think when I'm starin at your butt!"

"Maybe if I wore baggier clothes then…"

"Shh" Jack interrupted. "I'm having a light bulb!"

Jack used the term light bulb to describe any thought he had which involved money and its collection. It meant that all non- light bulb discourse must cease immediately.

"Wouldn't it be cool if we could make a gajillion dollars by selling stuff that's actually free for the taking but no one really understands that so they'll pay us to take care of it for them?"

"Sure Jack" Jill said, "That'd be dreamy." Jill had spent her childhood in front of the television watching old movies in black and white. "Dreamy" was her favorite expression, followed closely by "we now conclude our broadcast day".

Jack started waving his arms as he did every time he had a light bulb.

"We come up here for a pail of water every day right? And why? 'Cuz people are just too lazy to get their own damn water right? And…" he paused to let Jill chime in, because he loved that his girl was so smart.

"And people are always thirsty, right Jack?"

"That's right precious! They are! Let's go!"

And so Jack and Jill ran back down the hill without so much as a drop of water, but with a plan! Jack rented the old Hasenpfeffer place so as to have control over the 25 x 50 foot pole barn on the property. Then he hired Jill's brothers Flim and Flam to dig a secret tunnel up the hill, just below the surface of course, right to the old spring that flowed atop the grassy knob. After installing a pipeline in the tunnel and a spigot in the pole shed, Jill contacted Mister Breakweather the dumpster diver and contracted to buy all the bottles he could collect. Labels were printed, sporting a lovely logo; "Jack and Jill's Wondrous Water" it said, topped by a little drawing of a cute girl and boy with a pail clutched between them.

Well, it didn't take long before Jack and Jill's Wondrous Water was all the rage, first in Hilltown, and then, the world. Jack had done what all good Republicans must do to prove their Republicanism; get something for nothing and sell it for lots and lots of money.

Jack and Jill became billionaires. Jack was listed near the top of Forbes' top earners list and once in control of all that money he only wanted more yet. So he invested it all in real estate and a new product called derivatives. Soon, Jack became so stinking rich he was called "The King of Wall Street!" Jill would have been right there beside him as his queen, but fortunately or unfortunately as the case may be, she had, being a woman and therefore adverse to risk, plopped some of her free gotten gains in US treasury bills, just to hedge her bets, and that slow moving investment kept her from becoming the richest woman in the world.

This of course was 2007, when all the world was aglow and cash flowed from the fountains at every bank on the planet. Then came 2008.

Jack fell down
and broke his crown
and Jill came tumbling after.

Bedsnakes

SNAKE!!! I shouted the word just as I flailed the blankets off my chest (and off her's in the process), and knelt upright in the bed. **Get BACK**! I moved forward to protect my woman, setting myself as the only target, my hands open and arms wide in order to stop the monster if it was to attempt passage.

It was the first night Linda and I had slept together; the sex, wild, lengthy, exhausting. My house in the city was small and old, the corners dark. The urban noise seeped through its lath and plaster walls as if they were cardboard, the stained glass windows broadcast prismatic, creeping shadows as cars passed on the icy streets. It could be a spooky place if you let it be; the previous owner had died in it and some people couldn't swallow that thought without choking on it.

My bedroom, a relic of my divorce, was sparsely furnished...bed, frame...umm bed...frame...

I'd turned the real bedroom into an office once my ex had stripped me of my possessions and dignity; and utilitarian that I was, I moved my queen sized bed and frame into the tiny room to the front of the house. Between the radiator, the window and the entry and closet doors, there was really no place for anything else anyway, beyond a few sailboat posters and the standard single man dust bunny herd.

Linda and I had dated a few months, I'd written her poetry and read her Poe; what was left besides sex? She hated driving into the city, she was a country mouse and the nutcases I called neighbors scared her and her family as well. But she'd already seen me naked, an accident caused by walking up on me as I was suana/swimming at our shared campsite during our first canoe trip. I was unaware that her long walk alone had ended prematurely so I was devoid of my usual petty modesty. Something about seeing my non chicken legs and non concave butt made her crazy, and more than willing to follow me home to witness the remainder in person.

We'd spent all night at it; not easy for a man out of shape who smoked like a chimney. Once we'd finished, there was nothing left for snacks or chit chat; or even a quick cig for an incorrigible addict. We'd passed out cold and slept the sleep of the dead... *until the snake.*

It-*was*-**Huge**! A Boa maybe, or Anaconda! Luckily I'd spotted it out of the corner of my eye as I sometimes slept with an eye or two partially open. And now as it began to slither onto our bed, I took to my role as savior, martyr, knight in nakedness, and leaped to the fore to protect my lil darlin, my new playmate and wife in training.

Being a light sleeper and in a new and mildly uncomfortable setting, Linda was already half awake when I shouted; so jumping out of the way to cower in the corner was not a problem for her. She tells me that I knelt there for some time, looking from the back a bit like Jesus on the cross with my arms akimbo and my head tilted to one side...presumably listening for the hiss so I could target my enemy in the dark.

And then as she curled there, heart thumping wildly, sweat forming on her brow, I relaxed my formerly tightly strung musculature and lay back down, squishing my pillow into its customary position and reaching back to pull the slightest bit of sheet over my bare ass, as if a napkin would keep me warm. Within a split second I was "sleeping breathing" as she calls it, out like a light with a satisfied smile on my angelic, dimpled face.

For an hour she tells me, she just sat there shivering, asking herself ad nauseam if it was possible that a snake could just happen to be in the bedroom of a hundred year old house in a northern city in the middle of the coldest winter in a decade. Not only a snake, but a **massive** snake bent on feeding on human females.

She finally settled back to sleep as even fright couldn't stay her from lapsing into unconsciousness; the sex had just been too damn good.

When I awoke, I had no memory whatsoever of the snake, or even my heroism...Dammit! It happened once in a while, my Rem interrupted by some movement or shadow interpretation seen through my ever so slightly opened eyes. My first wife had once accused me of dancing in bed. I claimed I was putting on my underwear and was too stupid to do it on the floor rather than trying to stand on one leg at a time on a squishy mattress in the filtered light of the moon. But she might have been right. I only wonder whether I was any good or not since I don't dance when I'm conscious cuz I think I look stoopid.

I had to hand it to Linda; if she was able to withstand my sleepscreaming on our very first night together and still come back for more, how could I let her get away? You bet I married her, I'm not as dumb as I dream.

Ron Runeborg

Going Down?

It was drizzling and cold, and I would need to go from a doc appointment directly to work where I would spend the afternoon hopping in and out of a truck; so I'd worn my slicker, or Aussie cowboy coat for those hopelessly out of touch with manly man style. It's great gear for 'tween weather; not hot enough to make me sweat inside the truck yet plenty warm and solid enough to stop the frigid north wind.

I will admit, it only makes me look all that much bigger; and I suppose as it's Minnesota winter it might seem odd to some that I would be wearing oiled canvas cut in wild west gunslinger style at all. But I'm not a creature of vanity, I rarely peek in the mirror to see if my hair is combed much less fashionable, so I wouldn't be the guy to ask if I looked particularly scary at the time. I'm a clothing utilitarian; I wear what works to protect my health against the elements.

My appointment was with a shrink, a nut doctor, a loony tuner, whom I was consulting among other reasons for insight as to what it is about me people think so unbecoming, if not altogether frightening. My first visit had been tinged with hopelessness. I'd felt obliged to fix my many glitches to honor my wife's request more than make my life a thing of beauty. I'd not really considered it helping me, but perhaps I'd learn a trick or two about constructing lip zippers and hand clamps, so I could stop the incessant waving my arms and screaming bloody murder after each perceived foul. But on this the second round, I actually felt a draw to the building, as if there might be something inside just for me; a life lesson all wrapped in "you're the best" paper, topped by a purdy blue bow and an address card signed …Love, Life.

So while I was not oozing joy, I wasn't smelling of sulfur as if I were a direct conduit to the lair of Baal either.

I was limping, ok I give you that. I have a disease that causes my hobble; it's not like I can turn it on and off. And with the limp comes an occasional grunt. I do try to keep that inaudible, but sometimes it slips out; when it feels as if someone's driven an iron rod through the ball of my foot I once in a while say "Urgh" or something to that effect. But beyond my personal struggle to walk there was no black aura emanating from my Aussie cowboy clad body... I swear, I looked in the glass as I swung open the door, there was no red glow coming from my hands or eyes.

I clomped to the elevator and pressed up, and three folks come into the office building behind me; two girls perhaps 18 and 25, and a guy maybe 30ish. The door opened, I stepped in; there's room for a dozen... they remain outside. Girl one chuckles, that nervous titter they do, like when they're caught by gramma playing with gramma's vibrator. The group kind of shuffles stage right, out of my periphery, as if their feet are tied together as participants in a three legged sack race.

I laughed. Ok, I laughed with malice. Ok, I laughed in a contemptuous fashion. I grant I couldn't have thought all I've written here in such a short time, but the gist of my reasoning was: they'd apparently impugned my character on the basis of my appearance alone, and let me know they were afraid enough of me to keep themselves off my elevator; just in case I might have a hockey mask and machete under my raincoat, if not a naked pelvis and a desire to show it off. I was befuddled and hurt and ridiculed and angered all at the same time, so I laughed, just a little, kinda quietly, but loud enough they could hear; in hopes I might make them feel like fools in return.

And then the door shut and I thought the circus over. But no. In their zeal to not waste any more precious time they thought to signal the next elevator, assuming they could still get quickly to their destination, yet not have to share a car with past Grotesquemeda of Moorsby Watch. The elevator though, had outsmarted them. It knew I hadn't left yet, and it didn't know I'm scary cuz it's just a fucking elevator and elevators don't have preconceived notions. So in the interest of saving energy, it just opened up my door again; and there they were with their jaws nipping their knees.

I have to imagine it was quite difficult to decide which emotion was more powerful and therefore the one to follow; their fear of my cutting them in half and feasting on their rent flesh, or being recognized as such cowardly assholes that they'd humiliate themselves by refusing to ride on an elevator with someone who likely just <u>looks</u> like an executioner, but is probably a toy rocking horse rosemaler. The embarrassment won out, but the fear never really left. They came into the elevator looking to me as if one torso with three heads and six legs, immediately moving to the right wall, never turning their backs (or its back, to retain the visual) and pushed into the fake wood paneling until it buckled under their (its) weight.

High school Barbie giggled again, while her elder counted the raindrops on her shoes, and both squeezed into the guy in the middle as if blobs trying to absorb his life force. He in turn nodded to me; that manly nod that says "I know you could eat me Mister Ogre sir but please don't and I'll be forever grateful". There were three floors and I'd already pushed button three. They didn't look at the controls and they didn't ask me to assist, obviously willing to go wherever I wanted to go, wondering only if they'd be alive and with limbs at the end of the ride.

It was over all too soon. The door sounded as if about to open and I eagerly said "go ahead", knowing it could serve as my good Samaritan act of the day so I'd be one up on the sin tote board. They muttered thanks en masse', sporting enough red in their collective faces to light a downtown Tokyo Coca Cola billboard. I wasn't sure if all that blood had risen in wait for its release, soon to be offered freedom by my giant gas powered pruning shears, or if they were somewhat communally embarrassed by being such a trio of unmitigated prigs. Either way, little miss Muffet wasn't four steps from my evil claws when she stutter laughed and mumbled about the weird guy they'd just had to endure, and as I left the confines of the death chamber I noted the six legged creature blasting around the next corner at a controlled trot.

I swear, I was in an ok mood that day; I didn't glare, I wasn't muttering to myself and his majesty's dog. I didn't have a clown nose, floppy shoes or my penis protruding from my coat. I just got on the elevator kids, just tryin to get a ride so I wouldn't need to walk up three flights. I would have shared the box with a herd of Antarctic Jackalope for all I gave a crap, I had other things on my mind besides chain sawed flesh. But for the next hour it was all I could do to quit thinking about it. I almost wanted to grab those three, haul them into my witchdoctor's office and say "ok, creeps; tell him what you just told me, only with me you said it silently or just under your breath. This time say it out loud as if you actually had the power of your convictions…

and let's find out what my problem is once and for all."

But I didn't of course; that would have actually scared them and it's more fun to have a reputation for something that doesn't exist. Besides, it's not really my problem; I'm just a target not a weapons designer.

When I was younger I'd ride my motorcycle up to any given stop sign or semaphore, and if there were a car in the lane next to me I'd hear the door locks slam down, over the noise of my unmuffled Honda 750. It was comical then, it almost made me proud. FTW, or fuck the world was my motto in the 70s; not because I thought the world had given me a choice in the matter (as I believed it had stuck its middle finger in my face long before I'd reciprocated), but because I assumed I could live without the assistance of any other human being, animal, vegetable or mineral so help me GOD! Now that I know I can't really, the slamming of door locks just makes me cringe, as it verifies my worst fears, adds to my self- loathing and justifies my desire to shut down. That said, I didn't take my reaction to that extreme on this day. I just let it go after whining to the doc, hoping to write a good tale about it later. I will never be able to control peoples' reactions to me; their bigotry, their innuendo, their unreasonable angst. I can only control how much I care. Now if I can just find that agitation thermostat so I know not to crank it up at times like these, I'll be making some real progress.

Then again... maybe it *is* a lack of healthy vanity. Maybe I just need to comb my hair more often.

One Yellow Rose

She sits motionless, her head cocked away from me; no doubt letting the swiftly passing countryside take her to places far from here. The bruise on her upper arm tells a story unto itself. There are three blue marks in series, someone hit her hard enough to raise blood; and random scratches lower yet say that she fought back with equal fury, probably surprising her attacker who tried to hold her still to no avail.

The girl's hair, as red as cherry wine, is unwashed and disheveled; not as if she'd been living out of a car, but more as if she'd been in a hurry and hadn't bothered with a morning shower.

I note her left hand lying in her lap, palm down and fingers outstretched. She's flexing it a bit, relieving a strain perhaps, or reliving an anxious moment. I can see the mark of a ring on her fourth finger, a band of white, puffy flesh amidst a tautly stretched hand tinted brown by machine made tan. Her knuckle on that digit is slightly scraped, making me think she removed her band in a flurry of emotion, without a care as to how much skin came with it.

All of this may be a pessimist's interpretation. Why her bruise might simply be from her bumping into a doorjamb that held three large petrified wads of chewing gum at shoulder height, the scratches caused by an overactive cat. Maybe she was late to work and had to rush from her apartment before coifing her hair… and the ring thing? I suppose she might have been playing with one of those Chinese finger puzzle things and could get the damn thing off before it made the area pale and swollen.

But there were two more clues that brought me back to my theory. There is a fresh scar on her earlobe, looking much like a round headed stick pin. She'd had a pierced ring ripped out. Yes, it may have been an accident. Sure, she might have been walking along down some city street right alongside a commercial building that had just had repairs done to its face, and a stray nail might have been poking from the façade at just the right angle that when she sauntered by, her loop earring, swaying out and in because of the perkiness in her happy step, suddenly slipped over the nail and her forward momentum made any recovery an impossible task… and zzzzip, out came the jewelry. But my guess was she was in a fight, probably with her boyfriend, or husband if I have the ring thing right, and in the scuffle her earring was removed by force, intentionally or no.

What makes me think all this? You'd assume it would be an addiction to soap operas or a fascination with drugstore romance novels. But it's neither. In the woman's right hand she grips the stem of a perfect, just barely opened yellow rose. No friend handed her that flower, it has no wrapping, not even a ribbon around its thorny stem. She'd purchased the rose for herself from a street vendor, that's clear enough. And that the rose is a somewhat unusual color makes me think she bought it with symbolism in mind. Again, I agree, it could just be she likes the color yellow, indeed. But nothing else on her body, not her scuffed shoes nor cotton socks, her rhinestones jeans nor her tie died top were in any measure, any derivative of yellow. No, she strikes me as someone who finds comfort in the metaphor, the silent statement, the secret sign that screams its message to the chosen few who understand, and to no one else.

A yellow rose has limited meaning, it's generally the friend's offering given to mark a particularly joyous moment in the life of the recipient. It can also mean jealousy and be sent as a sort of poison pen. I think this is different, off the normal path; I think she's bought this beautiful living thing to commemorate a new beginning for herself, a fresh start, a kind of wax seal meant to notarize her self-made contract.

My stop has come and she hasn't budged. As I step into the aisle to go I can't help but whisper "good luck lass, you'll be fine I'm betting." It's nothing save a weak encouragement from a random stranger, and yet I feel gratified to have noticed her pondering tomorrows, and the opportunity to toss in a single "don't be sad, you're not alone."

For just a moment I imagined her assuming I was some panhandling bum or worse, a train riding lecher, *"eyeing little girls with bad intent"*. (Whenever I try to commiserate with a lost soul of the opposite gender I dread possible reprisal based in fear because my gender has made a mess of things since time began) But this time I'm lucky; she smiles as I pass, sucking in a short breath as if to say "was I that obvious?" And then she says "thank you so much."

I step from the train with a burning in my soul, I've done a good thing I think, whether I'm dead on about my supposition or slightly askew. She needed a kindness and she'd moved me to lend her one by simply carrying a yellow rose. Someday I may need to buy one for myself.

.

Ron Runeborg

Gods of Grape Juice

It's been a few millennia since monsters plied the seas;
since the world was more a pancake than a ball
Then lived gods of every discipline, of pointed expertise;
every pantheon appeared a cattle call.

There were gods of grape and orange juice, and gods of
golden toads; there were deities with several arms and legs!
Every country had a god of war immortalized in odes
penned as offerings from its own mortal dregs.

But now within our modern world we have but two or three.
(and an argument that they might be but one)
What happened to the others? Are there piles of god debris?
Don't they know that having lots of gods was fun?

If you had a thing for oceans, say, Poseidon'd be your guy;
not a generalist that covers all the bases.
It was cool to have the Valkyries come calling when you die;
not a chanting cleric mumbling of god's graces.

It's the wonderment that's missing, there's no drama to be
had; there's no plotting and conniving in the heavens.
It's just "happiness and gaiety, rejoice! Let's all be glad!"
Never "Zeus kills Aries! See it at eleven!" (s)

There was something grand in worshiping a multitude of
gods; disillusionment in one was no big thing. You'd just
dump that hack and choose anew from bevies of old sods.
Having faith was less "one spouse" than "summer fling".

Yet in this present century the pantheons have fled.
Here, the "one true God" is claimed by each in turn.
Far too many of those followers will make the streets run red
on the notion that non devotees should burn.

It's a bitter pill I swallow, one devoid of candy coat
to believe today means everlasting love.
I have lost my own ability to honor and devote.
I am lost within the singleness above.

You Are What You Eat

Morden stood atop the embankment searching the horizon in search of the enemy. He knew they were out there, he could feel a presence, and yet he could spot no movement at all. He tried to remember his aunt's favorite scanning spell, and finally recovered the words. In a moment the young mage had recited the "Butterfly's Eye", and suddenly he could view 12,000 pinpoints, each a focus unto itself. He took a new look at the space before him, concentrating on each facet in turn, and still discovered no creeping warg or camouflaged orc. He did though spot a delicious stand of beebalm in the near distance and began to drool ever so slightly.

Damned Straight

Lucifer shuffled into God's office and took a seat in the cushy leather chair facing the owner's desk. The Almighty was busy finishing up some paperwork, so Luc peered west through the floor to ceiling windows, admiring the naked female that was running here and there seemingly without purpose.

"Who's the chick?" he asked.

God looked up from His notes, pulled His glasses down to the tip of His nose and looked outdoors. He smiled. "Oh that's Eve" he replied, "I made her to keep Adam company; not that you need to know" he added as he set two sheets of paper before him, both facing his subject.

"OK" Luc said "I screwed up, I shouldn't have fought you, I get it. So what's the punishment then, let's get it over with."

"You have choices to make my child. Read each contract and agree to that which suits you best."

The devil picked up the first page and browsed through it, mouthing the words as he went. "Exile…own universe… far, far from here… uh huh, uh huh." He set that paper back on the desk. "You know" he said" you have very feminine script. Now that's not a bad thing, I'm just sayin…"

God looked downward and shook his head. "You can never quit can you" He said. "Read the other please."

Lucifer grinned, then shrugged. He was hoping to get at least a smile out of the Father, but there wasn't much humor in heaven, so he couldn't be too disappointed in the audience response. That didn't make him unfunny of course, just out of place. He reached for the second page and read aloud.

"I, Lucifer, Fallen Angel and scourge of heaven, shall reign over the fires of damnation for a period not to exceed infinity." He stopped for a moment and grinned again. Heaven wasn't humorless after all. "Nice touch that" he said, and then settled back into the chair to finish in silence.

"Ok" he finally said, "by the looks of it, were I to accept this punishment I will forever be your foil, like an open wound you can never heal. Why would you do this to yourself much less to me. I do love you ya know, I just got a little big for my britches there for a minute."

"Can't tell you that, sorry. It's a personal thing. Call it part of a plan, yin yang, a teeter totter."

"Teeter totter?"

"Oh you know what I mean, that's the best metaphor I can come up with at the moment. So you've read them both. Choose."

Lucifer didn't like either option really. All his friends were in Heaven, boring lot that they were. And God was always mucking about creating something, like that Eve chick. Man was she a hottie! If he left, he'd lose access to being the first to see all the new stuff. Suddenly his eyes caught another piece of paper, mostly because God was slowly sliding it away from its position on the desk, and whistling.

"Wait a minute! What's THAT! Another offer?"

God stopped moving the piece. "Well, it was" He said, "until you called my most perfect creation a chick. Do you have any idea how disrespectful that is? And I saw the way you leered at her with lust in your heart. Disgusting!"

"Oh Come on! Don't be so touchy, for your's sake! I apologize. She's a beautiful piece of work she is. Just like chickens. I was just comparing her to another of your most fab creations! And it was just an innocent glance! There, better? Now, let me see that other choice."

"Not a chance Blackbeard, you gave up that possibility by your snotty demeanor and lack of moral underpinning."

Lucifer stood and quickly turned toward the window, waving his finger toward the orchard beyond the meadow. "Why is… is that girl picking an apple?"

God jumped up from his desk and ran to the glass. Meanwhile, Lucifer grabbed the last paper from the table and started to speed read its contents. God, knew what had happened immediately, well, even before that really. And He was not amused.

Lucifer cried out. "You'd have forgiven me? We could have started over? I could have stayed? And you were gonna chuck this choice just because I called your beloved Eve a chick? Man! That's just not fair!"

"I don't have to be fair. I'm God" God said as he retook his seat and held out a fountain pen. Just sign one of these and move on Luc."

"That's just crap" Lucifer said, "You're the only guy I know that gets to be all loving and all vengeful in the same breath! That's Absurd!"

"It's not absurd" the Almighty answered, "it's a mystery."

"Mystery my ass! It's a conundrum!

"Oh alright, it's an enigma then."

"You call this an enigma? Bull! It's an impossibility is what it is!"

"And that's why you have to go my child. You just can't accept that some things are based entirely on faith. Choose, or I shall have to choose for you."

I choose that one" Luc said, pointing at the third paper he'd now dropped on the floor. "I choose starting over. I choose forgiveness. I choose love."

God's face was saddened, but His mouth firmly created the words "not that one" as he pushed the other two options toward his once favorite angel.

Lucifer wiped his tears, nodded, and said softly, "can you give me a minute alone? I just want to think. Really, just a couple minutes."

"Surely" said God, "take a stroll around the garden one last time. You have 15 minutes. I'd give you longer but I have a canyon I need to gouge out."

Lucifer shrugged and exited the room. The moment he shut the door, he began to hum and walked toward the huge apple tree deep within God's orchard.

He knew the chick was close by; he'd been glancing at her all through his conversation with the boss.

"Hey honey" he shouted as he closed in on the tree and maiden, "come here a sec, I've got a gift for you."

Eve flounced toward the lovely angel, tilting her pretty head and smiling a great big smile. "A gift? For me?"

The devil reached into the apple tree and yanked the biggest, juiciest apple he could from a lower limb, shined it up upon his feathers and offered it to the lass.

"What's this" the girl asked as she grasped the huge fruit.

"It's a Pop Tart" Luc said. "You could eat it just like that, but I'd warm it up first and share it with your boy toy. Pop tarts are best shared ya know."

"Well gosh" Eve whispered in awe, "I didn't know we had Pop Tarts in the garden! All I knew is that we're not supposed to eat the apples off the tree of knowledge or whatever, so I avoid fruit altogether. Adam says that's why my teeth are kinda falling apart!"

"Yea well, whatever dear" Lucifer said. "Now make sure you eat it all up or the Father will think you don't appreciate Him!"

"You bet Mister angel" Eve said, "I'm gonna go find a toaster right now!" And off she ran for the Heavenly kitchens.

A half hour later God stepped into the St. Michael's Bar, ordered a Smith and Currans and took a seat next to Lucifer who was sipping on a whiskey in a dark corner of the room.

"I was so miffed that you never came back, I might have dug that canyon a little deep" He said. He kicked at the suitcases that Luc had placed near the table. "I see you're packed. Which contract son, not that I can't guess after your latest hijinx."

"You're gonna regret this ya know. I'm gonna make life very difficult for your new little toys," Lucifer said as he signed his eternity in Hell into being. "Some people can deal with rejection. I ain't one o-those people!"

"So mode it be" God answered as He took the contract and slipped it into His letter jacket pocket.

"What the hell does that mean, so mode it be?"

"I don't know" God said, "it comes up in a movie in a few thousand years. I thought it sounded kinda cool so I co-opted it in advance."

"Well, I suppose it's yours like everything else is" Luc said as he stood and shook the Father's hand. "We'll see you around I guess. I'll send you a calling card now and then, like a disgraced Pope or something, just so you know I'm still in fine spirits."

"I'll never forget you Lucifer" God said with a tear in His eye.

"Damn straight" said Luc, and he turned and took the downward spiral of the stairway to heaven, never to be angelic again.

Thief of Thrones

If I were now to make amends for all the things I've done
I could purge until I'm ninety and know then I'd just begun
One could hardly say a good boy
found his way from mother's womb
I'm the rotten apple of her eye, the ass in her assume

Oh the blackness, it surrounds my heart
as white surrounds your rice
Why on Santa's list it's permanent, I'm naughty, never nice
When I'm faced by daily choosing I choose evil every time
If I liked it, it was nasty, if I loved it, 'twas a crime!

Oh I'm dancin' on the devil's grave cuz Satan ain't to home
he is messin' with some dressed up guy
who hangs around in Rome
In the meantime I'm his adjutant, his substitute depraved
I'm the thief of thrones, the dirty dog, the badly misbehaved!

Love is Blue

My mother's mother was a saint. Oh she wasn't beatified or anything, we couldn't afford to bribe any Cardinals for that treatment, but she was almost perfect in every way, except for that one thing. I didn't know about it 'till later in life, perhaps even after she'd had a debilitating stroke and couldn't have defended herself if she'd felt the need. But my mother told me about it, and I believe at least one of her sisters verified it. Gramma had a teeny weeny potty mouth.

I never heard it, but I wasn't looking for a language other than my own, so it may well have wafted past my ears a hundred times for all I know. See, gramma was born to a second generation German man and Irish woman who lived in a town that was predominately German and Catholic. She spent her first 8 years of schooling, I've been told, attending a German language one roomer on the outskirts of Waconia; so obviously she was well versed in Deutsch Sprache. Just before she died I was taught a phrase in German to say to her, and was incredibly gratified that she not only knew what I was saying but she smiled in response; but until that time I had no idea that she'd spoken a different tongue. I'd always thought it was cute that she pronounced some words funny, like Thdee for three, but I pinned it on her age, not her ethnicity.

I realize this is a verbose "explanational" prelude for something that doesn't even concern her specifically, but I'll finish by saying my mother once related to me that her mother used to say Scheisse when things went wrong or in the throes of some frustration. Once my mother figured out her saintly mom was saying "shit", she felt a lot more comfortable with her own swearing; and yet, in spite of her mental illness, in spite of her thinking my dad was the spawn of the devil, in spite of her losing her teeth at 30 and contracting emphysema at 32 and thinking her sisters hated her and on and on and on… she'd never once said a really, really bad swear word.

Yes she said damn here and there, and shit often enough, and asshole for my dad and sometimes she'd mutter son of a bitch, but she never got really vulgar; until I drove her to it.

It wasn't actually my fault. Not totally. I mean sure I used to say it around her because I was a badass teenager and that's what we said. Later in life I did my best to control it in front of women cuz, you know, women… and stuff. I never said it in front of gramma, even though she said shit and I spose she'd have learned to live with it cuz we were both being sinners and I'd already been tossed out of first American Pope school so I probably wasn't goin to heaven anyway; but still, she was gramma ya know? So no "fucks" in front of her; but mom?

I admit it did make me feel kinda oogy, and I didn't do it for the longest time, but then one day it kinda slipped out and even though she looked at me in that "if I still could I'd whip your ass" kinda way, the taboo had been broken and my fuckishness was set free.

Now I didn't use it all the time. It's taken me 50 years to perfect the fuck being every fifth word vocabulary; back then I only used it as intended, for things that could be described in no other fashion. Yet mom and I had many a conversation as she only slept a few hours at a time because of her COPD cough and I was up all hours because I loved the legal and illegal substances, so in the aggregate I probably said the word fuck in front of her a dozen times a day. Luckily, I think, she was so wrapped up in her own fantasy world she barely heard a word I said so to her. It must have seemed like I only said fuck a few times a day, and a few times could be forgiven.

I was always kind of amazed really; she was a woman who had every reason to swear like a sailor, her life was, in her mother's favorite naughty word, shit, for the most part. I thought it was cool that my mom kept to her Catholic upbringing in spite of her seeing little green men sometimes, and avoided all that verbal sinning. But then the stations of the cross came tumbling down.

She'd had a particularly bad bout with brain lotto. She'd shown me where in the newspaper the columnist had written about my dad and his philandering ways, and according to the article not only did everyone on the planet know it, but so did Ronald Reagan! It said so "Right There!!!" So, for the next few weeks I kinda gritted my teeth and tried to stay out of the way and let things slide and ignore the weird shit and all that jazz. But then, I was on the phone, talking to this girl… (understand, me talking to a girl was an event that rarely happened unless it was a friend whose pregnancy had reached the expulsion stage and I had to fill in for the father, whoever it might have been, in the labor room) …an actual chick who thought I was like a normal guy and while I realize that's awkward on its face, it became even more awkward when my mom yelled out and toward the phone "Is that another one of those whores you got pregnant?" like she actually thought I'd gotten anyone pregnant and if so it must have been a "whore"; or whatever was in her mind.

Well gosh, let me tell you I wasn't thrilled and if my gramma wasn't standing right there, having come over to help since my mom was on a tear and dad was hiding out at his folks, well I might have gone postal. But as I couldn't go postal in front of the woman who thought I'd be the Pope one day I just stomped out of the house and made a mess as I went, which I immediately felt bad for since I knew gramma would have to clean it up cuz mom would just sit at the kitchen table and stare at the mess while thinking about my dad in a porn movie he was making with Ronald Reagan.

It was the second time that happened that put me over the edge and changed my world forever. I was dumb enough to answer the phone one day, at least a week after the first time the phone had conspired to make sure I'd never have a girlfriend, when I was talking to another girl, a different girl than the first one although a friend of hers who was told by the first girl to stay away from me cuz me and my family were really crazy. And as I'm on the phone with this girl making kinda phone goo goo eyes like one does, forgetting all about the fact that our only phone was in the kitchen which was the lair of the beast and eventually she showed up all cranky like and while she didn't point out any other stories about my dad or any presidential porn proclivity she did start shouting at me something about my being an ass and if that's a girl on the line she must be a you know what and the girl started talking gibberish like she could hear what was going on and she just wanted to pretend our connection didn't exist and I finally hung up cuz there was no point, this relationship was going to the same nowhere all the other ones had and I shouted "FUCK YOU MOM, JUST FUCK YOU!" and she stood there for a minute all stunned like and then she got right in my face and shouted "FUCK YOU TOO!"

I slipped in and out of reality. My mom had just said fuck for the first time. A few years later a song on the radio would remind her of a time she experienced and while I was driving her downtown to shop she told me that she and my dad had once "done it" in a rocking chair.... so this wasn't the only time in my life that my mother had made my head swivel 360 degrees... but it was the first.

I looked at her, my eyes wide, and she kinda smiled a little, like with just the corners of her mouth. I was pissed beyond belief but I admit I was also a little bemused. I said "did you just say fuck you?" She stared at me for what seemed one full gestation and delivery, and then she kinda giggled and said "Yea. I did didn't I."

I said "do you even know what that means?" And she said "I'm not stupid. Fuck you. Fuck fuck fuck!".

We both laughed; that uncomfortable laugh when you'd really rather kick the snot out of someone at least metaphorically but you can't because it was pretty damned funny and all the strength gets sapped out of your hatred and you just stand there and kinda giggle.

"Don't do that to me again mom. I don't speak to whores, don't call my friends names. If you're mad at me fine, but don't crap on them." She said she was sorry, kinda mutter like, and then went back to her cigarettes and coffee and doodling a bajillion little triangles, and I went outside and smoked a pack at once and swore to GOD I'd never forget to never ever take a call at my parent's house, which I forgot within minutes of course.

To my recollection, she never said fuck again. She said shit a million times. She was her mother's daughter after all. But I had moved out before her next serious episode and while she was on planet earth she loved me just fine and never thought my friends were whores.

I've felt a little guilty over the years, that it was me that made my poor dear mom say the f-bomb. As she was a believer and surely went to heaven I've no doubt that her saying fuck led to a few years in purgatory, and it was all my fault she suffered. At least I am secure in the knowledge that I am to blame for nearly everything, so even though it's my mom we're talkin about here, my baggage concerning her is just another log on the fire, so to speak.

I miss mom. I'd even love it if she showed up for a minute and all she said to me was "fuck you". Cuz I'd know exactly what she meant by it.

Boo-Boo

I had a little boo-boo, and showed it to my mom
I told her I was beaten by our rotten neighbor Tom
She kissed my little owie and she said "I'll fix his wagon"
She got her favorite blowgun and her poison storage flagon
She told me "call the coward"; I did as I was told
I stood outside and shouted "Tom's a booger made of mold!"
Tom came out to challenge me; my mom took careful aim
She got him right between the eyes, his hair burst into flame
And now my boo-boo's better, while Tom's has just begun
he changed his name to Molly and he's off to be a nun
so let this be a warning to those bullys that I've known
I have a mean old mommy, and she'll make you creeps atone

Here's my Handle Baby

He is sleek, brassy, his body has incredibly classic lines. He looks like a Greek god, or perhaps a Roman centurion; he's powerful, aggressive, with a wide stance and broad shoulders.

I on the other hand am just a little teapot, short, stout, reflective. Sure I have purpose, I'm not just a fancy curio; though where I sit is generally reserved for pretty things that simply exist, I actually have a job in this family. I provide tea at the most formal of gatherings; I am in fact very well thought of in the household. I've heard many ooh and ahh as I'm lifted and tipped, and never have I dripped after a pour; my spout is flawlessly designed, my silver exterior perfectly polished. You'd think I'd be happy.

But it's lonely being exquisite, and until he showed up, I was quite singular in my magnificence. And then, "a new lamp!" she squealed; the mistress as amazed as I with the arrival of this wide brimmed stud with his translucent shade and his greek keyed, four footed base. The woman of the house couldn't keep her hands off him, stroking his fob, toying with his fringe, running her lithe fingers up and down his fluted shaft. I was insanely jealous, and immediately upon her leaving the room I tried to gain his attention so as to make him forget the hussy's advances. But for all my toots and clanks, I haven't yet gotten him to cast me so much as a sidelong light; it's as if he doesn't even recognize the other semi-inanimate objects in the room at all. I'll get him though, if I have to blind him with a reflection of his own gaze, he will be mine one day.

Addicted To You

Compacted to barely half her normal size so as to become nearly invisible, Melinda waited for the footstep to echo its last ca-lomp before racing down the long, granite hall. Following the right base, scurrying past barred openings that reeked of the foul, murderous creatures and their toiletries, she turned once right, and then twice left before reaching the door to her destination.

The box was still there, she could see it across the vast expanse; its blue, pebbled contents crying out to be stolen and put to good use. But the guards were about as well, and the swampers, waving their sodden mops to and fro, creating shallow lakes and riverlets that Mel would need to cross to claim her prize.

She was so hungry she nearly passed out watching the activity in wait for an opening. It had been days since she'd had her own meal, and her recent activities were only exacerbating her stamina problems.

Mel couldn't remember how long it had been for sure, but it must have been a week or more since Dophan awoke from his customary one hour sleep, sweating and smelling of molt. So at least that long she'd been running this course, bringing back whatever morsels she could find in the *creature kitchen* to feed her prince and protector while he was unable to do for himself.

He'd found the box on his own while on his daily scamper and once having tasted of its pungent contents, he was hooked. Mel had brought him various morsels and droppings in the first days of his sickness, but he'd have none of it, whining constantly that he would only eat the blue pebbles, that nothing else could save him; nothing else would make him happy.

Mel could only sigh at first, not believing her mate would allow himself to perish before he'd eat ordinary food. "Men are all pretty much alike", she'd been told by her mother; "they are brave and strong and unyielding until the moment they find themselves sniffling, and then they whine and moan like newborn".

Heeding mama's warning, Melinda was stubborn at first, facing off with Dophan's stubbornness and accusing him of putting her at great risk as some kind of silly test of her love.

But over time it was obvious that her sweet, sweet Dophan had some sort of addiction to the blue crumbs, and regardless what threats there were to her own safety in collecting them, it was her solemn desire to satisfy her lovely mate as best she could *in sickness and in health* as promised.

Hyperventilating, the young girl picked a path and threw her weight forward, tossing herself into the open light so as to remove her cautious reluctance by physical force. She ran as the wind runs upstream on a quickly cooling late summer's night, following her nose while her eyes were constantly darting across the horizon for signs that she'd been noticed.

She made the trip uneventfully save the splashes of soapy water on her belly, matting her fur and sending a slight chill into her anemic bloodstream.

The box was in its normal place, just under the shiny steel counter where trays of silver utensils waited for hundreds of thick, unclean hands to snatch them from their rest. It was dark near the box, and a bit scary if you'd ask Melinda; she'd already fought off an encroaching spider intent on laying eggs in her husband's foodstuffs; and as she was deathly afraid of the chitin jawed creatures, Mel had damn near died of fright before winning the day.

But love is an inspirational master, lending courage and prowess in battle to the weakest of its captives. And love was all Melinda needed to stay focused on Dophan's recovery.

She'd not yet told him they were expecting, he'd no idea how important it was that he become the same lord and master that he'd been before coming down with his virus or whatever it was. She couldn't do this parenting thing alone and he would just have to get better soon so as to pull his weight while she suckled the children.

A loud clank roused her from her restful but tense daydreams. The swampers were done, putting away their equipment in the maintenance closet and if she didn't hurry, the doors would close and leave her trapped until the next creature meal; too long for Dophan to live without at least a morsel of his precious pebbles.

Mel pulled back her lips and clamped her front teeth around two of the cylindrical pellets, careful not to touch either with her own tongue and start the melting process. If the food was to begin dissolving in her own mouth, she'd need to swallow and swallowing on the run always led to choking, then dropping the food, then panicking that she'd been seen and then starting all over again; so, better to keep her mouth totally dry for transport.

The floor was clear, the door still open. She pushed off the wall behind her for a tiny speed advantage and flew across the black speckled, white wasteland faster than she'd ever run in her life; and all to no avail as a shout and burst of wind from a misaimed mop gave her plenty of notice that she'd been spotted and was now in a race for her life.

The clomping was dreadful; multiple creatures were on her tail, one of them slamming his mop across her back trying to capture her in its cotton tentacles. Slowed but not stopped, Mel kept running along the wall knowing that to deviate from the path would surely spell her eventual doom in a place unknown. The creatures behind the bars were now joining in the chase, in spirit if not by foot. Their loud caterwauling was unnerving to the tiny lass; screams of **kill it, kill it** were frightening enough, but the taunts about catching her and making her a pettable slave nearly made her leave pellets of her own in her wake.

Looking up and away from her path in order to gather bearings, Mel made the last left and finally spied the crack she and the Dophan called home. She was winning this race, the mop monsters slowed by their sedentary lifestyles. *It has to be hard to keep fit* Mel thought as she sucked in her breath to form fit the sliver of doorway to her dusty but warm and dimly lit manse, *when you're cooped up in a box no bigger than your body all day.*

Once inside, she collapsed to the floor, spitting out her packages before huffing and panting her way back to a near regular heartbeat. She whimpered in the direction of Dophan, dreaming that he'd suddenly recovered while she'd been gone and was at this moment preparing to whisk her into his arms for butterfly kisses and baby talk words of his devotion, just before laying by her side in a bout of serious lovemaking.

For what might have been 20 minutes she lay there in silence with her eyes closed, imagining her lover's fingers slipping between the cold, hard floor and her warm, fuzzy spine. A few times she'd even held her breath in joyous excitement, the vision so strong as to make her truly believe that her fantasy was no illusion at all but actually occurring.

But as disappointment settled in to obscure hope, Melinda reluctantly opened one eye and peered toward the family bed, knowing that to do so was to destroy the possibility of her dream for good. And oh, it did more than that.

With a great wail Melinda stood and lept the few inches to her darling prince's side, touching his open jaw where spittle was oozing from within his stiffening body. Her heart stopped for what must have been eternity as she gazed upon the form of her only reason to be alive, the last vestige of her pride and comfort, the only mouse she'd ever loved.

A multi-image collage of their lives together drifted in and out of Melinda's fog, her tears flowing like spilled wine, always sippable off the alcoholic warden's kitchen floor. She lay across her *little Dope's* body, hoping that a lightning bolt might pierce them both and send her along with him to heaven.

Certainly God could see her pain! Surely the Almighty would take pity on this poor faithful and always tithing waif, so dedicated to her vows that she'd risk her very life to feed her dying husband a stupid blue pebble of smelly vegetable compound! **Take me, Take me PLEASE!** she shouted to all that is holy, but as always, in vain.

Dejected, trembling, the slight wisp of a girl sat upright on her haunch to ponder her future. She'd not seen another mouse beyond the magnificent Dophan in years, it was hardly likely that she'd find another mate in time for the birthing.

She could search beyond the boundaries of their territory to see if others were still scurrying, but there was always the risk that she'd lose her way and forever run like a rat in a maze, never finding satisfaction, much to the cursed *creatures'* entertainment.

A hollowness washed over her, not from her lover's death, not from her being quite alone, but from her absolute hunger, the pangs of which were now gnawing through her very righteous misery.

Mel sighed a heavy sigh; there was nothing to eat save the blue packages she'd nearly been squashed for. And there was something about them that made her queasy. Perhaps they looked all too inviting; were she to develop the same addiction to them as Dophan, she might lose her girlish figure and never attract a potential mate; not to mention have a severe liability if ever she needed to outrun the creatures again.

Then again, it was a long way to the kitchen; if this became the food of choice it would take oodles of energy to collect; and the scampering alone would keep her trim.

Almost absentmindedly she picked up one blue tube and began to gnaw on its upper end. She was again browsing her *library of memory* for photos and stories of her life under the protection of the Mouse Prince, and too occupied to notice that she'd eaten nearly half a pebble before being aware of its marvelous taste and texture.

As mice often do, Melinda set her troubles aside and bore into the chunk of chow she held in her tiny, clawed fingers. It was quite good, she was thinking...*No wonder Dophan would rather have died than eaten ordinary food, once having tasted* **this** *wondrous morsel.*

Wept out, pragmatically thinking of her next chores (move the body-clear the bed-get a good night's sleep-run for food-), Melinda munched away on her husband's last supper never had. She wanted to eat up and take her hour of sleep as quickly as possible. She had a whole new attitude about life now, moments after having been kicked to the curb by the powers that be.

She couldn't wait to run to the kitchen for more blue pellets, those things were damn good. Dophan was right and his teachings served his lover Melinda well; *if it aint spelled "Rat Poison"*, the Mouse Prince would always say, *it aint worth eatin.*

Of Curses and Cowardice

I was ashamed really, of both Donald and myself. The shame I took on at my own expense was justifiable, I had been silent more than once while my sometimes friend had been ridiculed in my presence; I'd not once lifted a finger, not spat a single "shut up" toward the crows who mocked him in his misery.

But the shame I felt for <u>him</u>, or for myself *because of him* was confusing, nearly debilitating. Whatever the curse that affected him, whatever the reason he knelt on the floor and barked like a dog, foaming at the mouth and inevitably wetting his pants, I should have been capable of understanding he was innocent, that none of this was his "fault". Or perhaps not then; perhaps I was just too young to absorb the concept that there is no shame in acting like an animal if it's not within your control, nor is it shameful to show allegiance toward that person, up to and including coming to their defense.

Though I couldn't intellectualize how I felt, instinctively I was positive that to leave him alone during one of his fits, to not stand guard so as to be sure he didn't hurt himself or suffer bullies' abuse would be a sin of a high magnitude; somewhere in between venial and mortal I guessed.

In retrospect I can see my path had been set already. My own worthlessness had deemed I was a perfect candidate to be a martyr; if I was going to spend my life being kicked, I may as well be kicked for good cause and have a ticket for the sainthood lottery. I became the keeper of the strays, the defender of the defenseless; at least in my mind. I did though have an issue; I was afraid of pain; I'd never learned to fight and the few times I'd not been able to boast myself out of danger I'd had my head handed to me. So, I was a coward by self-decree. Too afraid to run that my soul be damned by my refusal to be my brother's keeper, yet too afraid to fight lest I either kill someone in a blind rage, or suffer permanent scars. I so wanted to be a good person as defined by my romantic notions of "the way of the White Knight… yet when handed the opportunity to demonstrate my willingness to suffer slight in the name of right, I folded every time.

And here we were again, by sheer coincidence two fourth graders in the boy's bathroom together. Suddenly, down Donald goes, leaving the sink where he'd just worked up a lather and dropping to his knees, beginning to do that "chuff" noise as if he were coughing up a hairball. I stood close enough to jump in if I noted he was turning blue, yet far enough away that his disease not leap from his skin onto mine. In come three eighth graders, obviously in cahoots, looking to plan true mischief, or at least discuss breasts and baseball and maybe toke a single cigarette between them.

It started immediately, they moved in like a pack of feral dogs who'd found a butcher's dumpster, surrounding Don's quaking form and growling at each other, daring the others to eat first.

It must have been the gazillionth time I'd been given the challenge to ride into battle or hide with the children and cripples. I have to believe that for the first few moments as my blood flow stopped I "knew" what my response would be. That I'd pray to become invisible and ride out the storm a spectre; so pathetic a cur that I was unworthy of even a glance much less a foot in the ribs or the saliva it would take to spit in my face.

But something in that moment caught me off guard. In my mind I saw myself on the floor, barking, being pushed and laughed at and whistled for. And I exploded, vocally; and physically though within my own space. I launched into a speech about how I was insane and how I would come to their houses in the dark of night when even their drunken, useless, abusive fathers were passed out and I'd kill them all with scissors or fireplace pokers or even my fists if need be… unless they got the hell out of the bathroom right now and left my friend Donald alone. I screamed the words, and coughed the words; I pranced and kicked the wall as if I were trying to get a foothold so I could walk to the ceiling. I was every bit as large as the attackers, a gift of nature that kept me alive and unintentionally threatening into adulthood. So when I pounced around the room slamming my fist into my hand and my shoulder into the graffiti tainted urinal wall, I'm sure I made quite the visual; a sort of "Freddy Krueger in corduroys and a clip on tie goes to Catholic School".

I was still prancing when I noted the door to the lavatory was swinging shut and Donald was turning blue. I'd saved us it seemed, but only so this boy could die nearly alone. I dropped to my knees on the tile floor and rolled Donald onto his back, then sat him up into my lap, raised his head and reached into his mouth to pull his tongue out of his throat. His breathing caught wind and there we sat for a few minutes, he oblivious to his surroundings much less his name, and I, weeping, softly, for one of us, or more likely both.

In the end I determined I was a coward still, but with one defensive victory in my favor. Never satisfied, but gratified I'd overcome my own curse, if only that once.

Ron Runeborg

One Life Remembered

It was the only tree left standing of what was likely once a forest; an outcast, a loner, insistent on keeping its face to the sky and its feet firmly planted while hoping for the best. When the land was cleared for cash crops, one thin giant remained for no apparent reason. Maybe it stood as a living section boundary marker, or perhaps the owner thought it totally symbolic of the Christmas season, a reminder to keep the faith, the peace and thy neighbor's welfare in the forefront of his thoughts as he suffered the mundane tasks of day to day farming.

The road was named after it, mistakenly. "Lone Pine Road" they called the two rut cart track that beelined due south from Mushtown, passing the massive tree just before ending at a drainage ditch. Surely it was just an access road for the property owner to reach field A from field B, but once farming had become a corporate business and no longer the purview of individual entrepreneurs, the property was sold for a pittance to the rapidly encroaching city to be used as parkland, and the road became an "issue".

It's a common error, calling every tree with needles a "pine". It was a Norway Spruce actually, a bit over a hundred years in the making to my eye; majestic, a specimen of rare quality in spite of its lonely, solitary placement, sticking out like a sore thumb as it were.

I can't claim to know its history, only that it had one and it may have been more colorful than we would think.

It had been pruned up to seven feet by someone who wanted to use the shade below without attracting a face full of twigs. That would imply it was a destination, a shelter, for man or beast. It would have made a great picnic spot, well shaded, nearly hidden with lower branches drooping to touch a ground layered in soft brown needles, a coverless comforter on which to set an afternoon meal.

Hell, maybe there's an entire romantic twist to the story of Lone Pine; a young protestant Czech girl in love with a young Catholic Irish boy who were forbidden to see each other, but whose love was so strong they bolted from their beds at the stroke of one each morning, bound for the biggest shadow on the horizon, unmistakable even without the moon and stars to light the way...and maybe there under the swaying arms of the natural umbrella they made love, and promises, and planted the seed of a wholly new life devoid of their ancestor's prejudice and injustice.

To those to whom dreams are only the indecipherable stuff of the unconscious, I'm sure it was just a tree; big, ungainly, somewhat dangerous and always in the way. To the few of us, it was a pointy palace, an emerald banner, a post it note reminding us that being alone and unique can be beautiful... even awe inspiring to eyes that choose to travel beyond the tip of their owner's nose.

In my world it's silly to fight for a single tree unless it has some incredible tale to tell; even had I proof that some wonderfully anecdotal but non-historic event had taken place beneath its boughs I doubt I would have stood in a town hall and begged for its life. I would have lost anyway, the acres were being groomed as ball fields for the local children and there's no winning any argument once the word "children" enters the conversation. Besides, the tree was slated to remain intact; there was no standing order, (at least expressed in public) that the "pine" must perish.

Yet perish it did, though it took a lifetime to become a risk to humans and so it died little by little over four years before finally greeting the logger who then ended its misery.

It never surprises me that people know nothing about the cultural requirements of trees. Very few know anything of their <u>own</u> culture, and if they do they seldom travel outside that circle except to jam their wants and needs down the throats of others in the name of diversity. When people are so callous about people, it's hardly news that plant material is an absolute mystery to the vast majority.

Had someone simply taped off a reasonable circle wherein heavy equipment would be taboo, the lone "Spruce" would have sheltered yet more picnickers for many more decades. But the development was not about trees or wildflowers or history for that matter, it was about providing space for doting parents to scream at volunteers who baby-sit their kids by coaching them in some organized sport rather than teach them how to explore the world in their own way. The tree was an afterthought, a nuisance, too close to the road and the graders and pavers that suburbanized its rutted track.

I can't weep for the tree; that's silly. But I can see it as an example of people's myopia, people's self-centered greediness. There was no reason the Lone Pine had to die, there was every reason to keep it whole and healthy at damn near all cost, if truly city works are for the benefit of all taxpayers and not just the bleeders and takers and arrogant narcissists. But that's not the case. Parents in my experience are very squeaky wheels and their desires take precedence over all others save the wealthy. That said, a wealthy parent stands atop his or her peers even more so. Let no expense be spared.

It's called Lone Pine Road still, though there's not a conifer of any biological family in sight. Maybe someday some do-gooder will talk the city into planting a seedling as a tribute to the hundred years of living history that was ignored to death. Hopefully it'll be a pine, but I'd settle for a shrub juniper if that's all they could come up with; it's not easy reading plant research with blinders on, I get these people are not elected for their ability to spew Latin names of herbaceous species.

Maybe someday I'll sneak into the park in the dead at night, when all the kiddies have gone home to their x-box's and sodas, and the last coach has suffered his last insult and retired to the last saloon for his first beer. Maybe there I'll replant one of my own trees, dug out of my yard for the occasion on the knowledge that to have something done right, you do it yourself. Maybe I'll put a big mirror in front of it so it seems to disappear into the surrounding neatly planted, fake generic landscape, as if no one knows about it before it's too big to kill with ease, it may stand a chance.

It's funny to have written a couple pages in honor of a single tree. But maybe when I print it, the paper will know I'm referring to its grandfather's generation....and this time won't make the ink to smear like it usually does. One can only hope there was a point to this story.

Ron Runeborg

To Catch a Falling Star

Sheriff Ted Brownbear stepped from his cruiser and peered up at the ring of pvc. It was as tall as Bill and Sakaway's house and appeared to be a hundred plastic pipe elbows glued together to make a giant circle. Bill's grandson Johnny was teetering on an extension ladder, leaning out over the roof's peak, stringing copper wire and leather strapping to various predrilled holes. Then as Ted watched, the boy climbed down, slipped the two leads through a pair of lower holes and started up the ladder again, dragging the materials behind him.

"Your neighbors want to know if you're crazy and I should haul you off to the asylum John Eagletalon. What should I tell them then?"

Johnny laughed. "Tell them they're old and will strain their eyes peering from their windows! Or tell them to mind their own business."

"Now John" Ted continued; "you must admit this thing looks a little strange, are you makin' a space ship radio antenna maybe? Are they comin' to take you home?"

Both men laughed at that, and John hooked his wire over the ladder top and climbed down.

"I'm building a dream catcher if you must know."

The sheriff smiled. "It's supposed to be a little thing that hangs in the window boy, did your granddad put you up to this?"

"Here's the thing" John said as he stepped in next to the cop and lowered his voice; "I've been having some real nightmares lately; ever since I've been back from Afghanistan. I've been chased by massive spirits, gods maybe... even Kokopeli took a whack at me with his flute one night. Well, you can't stop a god with a spider sized dreamcatcher now can ya?"

Ted thought a moment as he looked at the circle and back again. Johnny was crazy alright, but it was a good crazy, a unique crazy, a storyteller's crazy.

"Go on then and build the thing, I'll tell the neighbors to pull their shades if they don't like it."

Driftwood

He sat alone on the beach, as he had during every holiday for every year as far back as he could remember; since the crash and fire that had consumed what had been his family. His eyes were sunken, his hair, matted. His skin was scraped smooth by the wind whipped sand that rose unto the sky in small whirligigs. Shoes missing, shirt torn and dirty, shorts wrinkled and sopping; he looked as if a piece of weathered driftwood, released from the earth, expelled from the sea.

Betty Lou's Impatience

Jack Billmore was not a good dancer, to that he would freely admit. But, as he would confide to his friends, his lack of grace should not mean that he'd be penalized for life; never having the opportunity to trip the light fantastic with the chick of his choice, or press chest to breast while wobbling about a polished tile floor.

That his father was wealthy helped his chances. Girls were reticent to turn down his requests, even though they were assured of leaving the ballroom with bruised ankles and scuffed shoes. It was simply a matter of economics. That was until Betty Lou Bablunski came to town.

Betty Lou had not yet been accepted into a Poncho Villa Middle School clique, and so had not heard of Jack's inability to walk and chew gum at the same time. It's no surprise then, when Jack asked for her hand during a school dance hip hop medley, she happily accepted, hoping her action would finally break the ice and see her popularity rise.

It wasn't until the sixth time Jack stomped on her right toes that Betty Lou felt compelled to warn her partner of her prowess in the pugilistic arts. Jack could only giggle; the idea of a 13 year old female boxer seemed so cute. That was his downfall, as while giggling he failed to watch his feet and kicked Betty Lou square in her right shin.

A gurney was needed to take Jack's limp body from the gym that night, and another for Bobby Phelps, yet another for Fred Wannamaker and a fourth for the principal, Mister

Hanks. Betty Lou had gotten her wish; at this dance she'd indeed broken the ice.

Face Paining

It was dark. It was cold. I was lonely but determined to have fun in spite of being a single moving object in a sea of snow and slush. The lights above the hockey rink a few hundred yards off gave me some cheer, and the sound of pucks slamming off the boards was romantic to a boy of seven. I thought about dragging my sled home to find dinner, it had to be after six o'clock. But then I figured there was no reason to walk, swishing my thick snow pant legs against each other as if trying to start a nylon fire. I could run, holding my sled off to the side until I'd reached maximum speed, hopefully at the border of the skating rink... and then slam my ride to the ground and leap upon the suppertime express. If I'd gotten up enough speed I'd probably get halfway across the park before I had to waddle the rest of the way.

I backed up a bit and positioned the sled, then ran like the wind. Just as I got to the rink I dropped my craft and jumped on its back, flying over the mogul that I hadn't noticed in the waning light. My vehicle and I separated and we both hung in the frigid air just one moment. Then both of us found the surface of the earth with our faces, the sled having a much easier time with the contact than I. I spent the next ten minutes spitting ice chips, and my best and brightest front tooth; the first of my adult teeth to free themselves from my always inhospitable jaw.

The Steel Mistress

Emil had never in his life received such an extravagant gift. It took three men to bring it into his home, and though he was as strong as three men, he could hardly lift it himself. Once the burlap covering had been removed Emil could do nothing but fall to his knees and weep. The edge was keen as a wolverine's claw, its surface so highly polished that any man standing between it and the sun would surely be blinded. King Richard had held true to his promise; working above and beyond the call of duty had paid off handsomely.

It was a week before the gift could be mounted and raised unto the sky, and another day before the first guest would stare in awe at its shiny new character.

"Please help me" said the young girl Jean DuForte, accused of heresy and other high crimes; "I am so afraid."

"Do not fear lass" replied Emil; "you are her first, she will make certain you feel no pain, I promise you."

Jean might have smiled if the executioner's assistants had not placed the slit block over her neck, forcing her face into a freshly washed wicker pail.

Emir tugged at his rope, and was barely able to mutter "God have mercy on your soul" before his guillotine's brilliant blade had tasted its first blood.

Eye of the Beholder

Johnny had finished his project and scurried to the desk of his teacher to request praise.

"Sister Mary Judas! I've finished! It's good don't you think?"

The aged nun studied the drawing for some time and then said, "Why red Johnathan? I've asked you to produce a painting demonstrating the color of sin and you've drawn a man covered in red!"

"It's the fires of hell surrounding the wicked man sister. If you sin you are consumed by hell and damnation! Isn't that so?"

"Yes John, it is so, but the sin itself is black; it makes a black mark on your soul. You can do better on this assignment. Try again son!"

Johnny hung his head, slipped his paper from the desk and returned to his seat... but was back within a few minutes.

"Alright John, let's see what you've..." Sister paused; "Why it's the very same drawing! I hope you have an explanation for this young man."

"I do Sister" the boy said; "This is my dad and for beating my mom and me every day God sent an angel down from heaven to rip all the flesh off his wicked, wicked bones, one strip at a time. This is a picture of him taken just before he's sent to hell where Satan will pour hot tar on him, turning him from red to black!"

The nun could only stare, her mouth, paralyzed, her wits scrambled.

"You said every work of art has many interpretations Sister" John continued; "you saw red, but I saw only darkness."

Mask Macabre

Well… he was good looking, seemed to have money, was as polite as any genteel southern boy I'd ever met, even though he was obviously a Yankee. I didn't approve of his driving a Volkswagen Beetle of course; not only was it a homely little car but it wasn't made in America and I damn well believe in buying American. But that was his only major flaw that I could tell, so I gave my approval to his dating my sister Darlene. And now she's missing; has been for a week. It's not like her to not at least call, even if this guy had swept her off her feet she'd have notified me or her mother as to her intentions if not her whereabouts; she knows we worry so.

His name? Yes, I have it written down. It's Bundy, Ted Bundy. Yes, I'll hold.

Once Sighted, Twice Dead

Dusty stepped from his back porch mud room onto the concrete stoop and took a long look across his driveway. He'd already moved the tractor, the line of sight was clear, and while the air was especially bitter this morning, he was dressed for a long winter's hunt.

Candice yelled to him from the upstairs bath window; the bath she'd been locked into all morning. "Don't bother calling today honey, I'm going shopping and I'll be gone all day."

"Yea, yea" he replied in his best caustic tone. The F150 started after a few tries, and with a lurch he turned toward County road Six and drove away. It was only a half mile to the turnoff, clearly within eyesight of the house if the occupant just happened to be looking in that direction from an upstairs window. Dusty knew he had to take that chance. His friend would be arriving within twenty minutes of his departure, and if he drove too far away to hide the truck, he'd never be able to walk back in time.

He slipped into a copse and parked near the picnic tree, the massive elm that his grandfather had landscaped around so as to have a secret garden where he might take his wife and children to celebrate special events. As he walked back toward the house, his eye was struck by a glint of reflected light, and for a moment he thought to cancel this whole affair.

Carved in the picnic tree was a heart, a foot tall if an inch. And at the base of the heart he'd carved a small dent where he'd pounded in his favorite polished quartz, a symbol of his undying love. Love at thirteen is like that, the fantasy that the stone was diamond was every bit as powerful as the fact that it was not; and once his true love had seen "Dusty loves Candy" carved into the heavy bark with the stone splashing prismed sunlight onto the letters as if an open air kaleidoscope, she'd been his from that day forward.

Until a few years ago in any case, and that memory wrenched Dusty's attentions back to his task and he began to trot toward the machine shed's rear so as to take his place.

He'd called it a deer feed, the pile of corn cobs and field trash he'd made between two outbuildings. Candy had argued for days about his moving it; she liked her yard neat and tidy. But he'd won the argument and in fact had made the pile a little taller once having tried it out and noting he could still be seen.

Now he dug his rifle from the snowpack where he'd buried it, slipped it from its case and checked for load and safety. He'd made it just in time, the Volkswagen Beetle he knew would be incoming as he was outbound, was just pulling into the drive.

It'd need to be one bullet if he could manage it, he really didn't want to chase anyone all over the house trying to ignore the screaming and pleading. The longer it'd take, the more likely he'd give up the quest, and he'd spent too many hours working up the courage, to ruin it by letting someone talk him off his high.

He needn't have worried; it was cold, but not cold enough to stifle passion. Candy met Jack at the door to the back porch in her bathrobe and obviously nothing else, and the two stood still for a long minute to reacquaint themselves to each other's lips. Through Dusty's looking glass, the crosshairs made a mark directly in the center of his best friend's temple, if he could wait just a moment, the two might turn that fraction of an inch that would make the job easy, less unpleasant.

As Dusty saw the scope fill up with hair and then the triangular "nape" of Jack's neck; he pulled the trigger, and ended three lives in the space of a single icy breath.

A Satin Wake

She was stunning, my Roseanne; a slight girl, barely reaching to my waist yet her powerfully feminine presence made her true stature immeasurable. Her hair was sculpted, layered black on black; perfectly formed as if the feathers atop a raven's wing. Into her eyes one could fall for an eternity; those bottomless wells of midnight blue now covered by lids heavy with the weight of the netherworld. She'd the nose of a little girl, slightly freckled, a tiny upturn, proportionate in the style of Michelangelo. Roseanne had the upper lip of a prayer; an odd analogy perhaps unless you can visualize the words earnest, passionate, joyous and well loved. She smiled even as her face lay in stasis; she was happy, always, even unto her death. Her lower lip was pouting, sensual, serious...

I kissed my first two fingers and then reached into her satin lined coffin and set them on that lip; the lip I'd touch while drawing her face close to mine back when we were young and in lust. "Goodbye darlin" I muttered. "See you when I get there. It shouldn't be long."

Ron Runeborg

Dinner for one, Breakfast for two

She dug her nails into my arm for the third time, oblivious to the pain she was causing me. I represented my gender I suppose; I deserved a flaying for being a random sperm carrier, as her *personally selected* sperm carrier wasn't present. In fact, he was only present when depositing said sperm was an option; the birth of his daughter would be an inconvenience so he'd decided to stay away and find an alternate repository for the time being.

"God, I'm starving" she said once she'd huffed and puffed and blown the room to shambles.

"Have my Snickers" I said, "but hurry up with it. I'm sure the doc's would throw me out if they knew I was feeding you candy during your contractions."

"Shuttup and gimme that" she said as she snatched the brown wrapper from my hand.

I stroked her hair as she damn near swallowed the gooey confection. She deserved better than this, and so did I. She deserved more than a friend at her bedside, and I deserved recognition for always being there; but neither of us was lucky enough to get our way.

"Promise me something" she groaned as her next attack began and her nails found purchase in my flesh.

"Anything kid."

"Bring me a cheese danish for breakfast."

"And for the baby?"

"She'll have her own dairy for God's sake, just bring me the danish!"

"Whatever your little heart desires" I pledged, as I watched rivulets of blood run into my palm and then drip to the floor.

Pane Turner

I stared out the library window, wishing I could simply reach into the pane and turn the page. It wasn't actually raining at that moment, but the air was so thick one could see it smear all the world's empty spaces; like the residue from a popped soap bubble sliding down a sheet of clear plastic. It had been a miserable week and while I love books and the old, solemn buildings that house them, I was damn tired of reading about things I could be doing if only the sky would explode and send its humidity back into the underground reservoirs where it belonged.

I could deal with a downpour, and I love a good thunderstorm, but the incessant mugginess made walking much like slogging through the flesh of an overripe grape. It was slow and sticky, it smelled too sweet and tasted a bit rancid; and it wrinkled the flesh as if acidic to the touch.

It was there, in that grape afternoon, that I first made the acquaintance of Edgar Allen Poe; another great whiner if I might be so bold as to put myself in His Vice's company...

Ron Runeborg

High Price to Pay (Just a day in the life)

The supper club was a manly man's affair; all dark wood and dusky paints, low lighting and many bottles of wine and spirits standing atop any available shelf like appendage. I believe we were first in the door, though second to be seated as Linda does so love to use the restroom in a public place. Cloth nappies, goblets, flutes and highballs adorned the leather clad booth, alongside various utensils that made clear this was no pancake house we'd strolled into.

There was a time, way, way back when I was a master of commerce and taken on the road as the local's resident business theater audio engineer that I would eat fancily schmancily on a regular basis. Meals of many names were served me, things Dianne, and stuffs Foster; place names like Chateaubriand and even sound effect foods like ratatouille (Imagine a cartoon machine gun spitting out tobacco juice). On the dole we called it. Expense account sounded so droll, and we were creatives for God's sake; we had to be slightly askew in every word and deed. While we were relatively conscientious we would occasionally break the bank and have ourselves a 100 dollar dinner for two, in spite of the fact that neither of us drank alcohol. I suppose if I were to total it up I'd have had a hundred fifty vastly overpriced but delicious meals a year for a decade or so. In fact I even got into the habit of taking people to those eateries on my own pocketbook as for a blessedly brief time in my life I believed my own hype and played the social strata game to suit.

In the end, as I had with most music, I burned out on excellent foodstuffs, and longed for nothing more elegant than watery oatmeal and peanut butter toast. I have to imagine the loss of half my income could in part account for my decision; it does tend to make a menu sporting 35-50 dollar entrées appear as if a list of items that taken together might make a lovely down payment on a house. And so when my boss, cleaning out his wallet one day while waiting for the time clock to clank 4PM, tossed me a supper club gift card he'd never used because the venue was just too highbrow for him, my first thought was of having to wear something other than sweat pants and t-shirt in order to use it, and not of how delicious the meal might be. I carried the plastic cash for 6 months, mentioning it only once to my lovely in passing, along with the whine about the change in clothing that would be necessary. And then, Valentine's Day arrived.

Now it's not as if we'd not commemorated the day and reaffirmed our deep as the big blue sea devotion to one another already. Card: check. Poem: check. Self-created haute cuisine celebratory meal: check. Yet, the little woman wanted one more show of fealty to her charms. She wanted... the supper club. She'd called to verify the worth of the gift card, she'd looked up the menu on line and she'd convinced herself that she just couldn't live without our spending an hour or two under the dim lights, supping on ambrosiatic victuals du jour.

Of course I complied; it is my duty to cater to all things Linda. I did pout a bit, and wallowed in a pool of dread while pondering the possibility that one of the two or three pairs of actual slacks that I own might still fit me after a dozen set-aside years. But as time went on and she became more and more enamored by the concept of fine dining, I resigned myself to making the evening as pleasurable as could be. As it turned out, one pair of slacks did fit, but only after putting every ounce of muscle I had in both my massive arms to the task, pinching the button into place just a whisker before my muscles began to quiver like Jell-o and my mind screamed for mercy. Of course, I'd forgotten to tuck in my shirt and so I had to go through the entire process again, this time almost giving in and relying on the old pants fastened by length of twine and long coat worn over them all evening trick.

At last we arrived at said establishment where the lady seemed in her glory. Even the water poured table side seemed a richer color, texture and thickness to her than that ordinary liquid we drank at home. This was the sign of a cheap date if ever there was one. She had planned on ordering "frikadeller", Danish recipe meatballs on a lovely bed of red cabbage, a treat from "the old country" her grandmother called home. But there was an issue. Frikadeller it seemed was an appetizer, and though one could have an appetizer for dinner, one would normally order an entrée so as to get one's money's worth while having one's hunger sated. It was a dilemma. Neither of us had more than a handful of dollars to spend beyond the card, so while you'd think in a club one would always have an appetizer along with dinner, followed by a dessert and perhaps an after meal libation, we were on the poverty plan. I did offer to hock my boots and the ice scraper from my truck in order to pay for her Danish delight, this being a dinner to prove my adoration and all, but she declined, and reminded me that I probably make better meatballs than they could, and that she makes better red cabbage. Sometimes pretty much everything in life is a challenge. Sometimes, it's like sliding down a mountain of butter; quick and easy... and tasty too.

She went for the Chicken Oscar, Oscar of course being a Scandinavian name and therefore likely related to the frikadeller making it a reasonable substitute. I had the Burgundy tips, which made me think of all the poor Burgundians running around Burgundy with their fingers shortened by one knuckle; an insight I kept to myself as Linda's romantic mood could be broken with too many "Me-isms". The Oscar was lovely (though not at all pickled as one would think), a beauteous combination of crabmeat, asparagus and Béarnaise atop a quite juicy chicken chestual appendange. My tips were also fine, an aromatic wine sauce on fingertips devoid of their distracting fingernails. A popover and salad completed the tour, golden water for her and coffee for me. Oddly enough there were leftovers, but only of the lettuce variety, or variety lettuce variety if you will pardon my verbosity, as the entrées were gobbled right up (to quote Goldilocks).

I have to admit it was a grand event; I told stories, she giggled, I flirted with the waitress, she giggled, I showed the maitre d' my checkbook balance, he giggled, a fine time was had by all. Still, I only hope I won't have to wear an actual pair of slacks for another decade or so. It's a little frightening at my age to conform, even for my true love.

Full Circle

I was positive I could touch the sky if only I could get enough momentum. I had the leg power certainly. If I could harness the timing of pushing off at just the right moment, and pulling the chains at the very second they reached their return point, I could propel the swing into a total circle and grab the stellar brass ring on my way by. The crossbar was at least 15 feet off the ground, the swing set, a heavy duty sort made of Pittsburgh steel and planted by men employed by the WPA during the depression. The seat was a leather strop, wider surely but much like I'd seen hanging from my barber's chair, used to put the finishing touch on his straightedge razor's blade.

I figured if I were fifteen feet above the crossbar I could likely touch a cloud or two. All things being relative, thirty feet is outer space to a kid that's only four feet tall.

So push I did, and within a few tries I had it down, bearing into the motion like a rower in a single boatsman race. Higher and higher I flew, past the center point where centrifugal force was beginning to loosen its grip on my slight form. I was a little scared, I wondered if I'd made a miscalculation as my ride became a bit more herky jerky. But I was so close, there was no way I could stop; the sky was just a few yards from my grasp. And then of course I reached a place of neutral gravity, when the only thing holding my plump bottom to the leather seat was a fervent wish.

I rocketed straight down at many more miles per hour than I could count at that young age. When I hit bottom I was still clinging to the chains, and the resultant snap not only whiplashed my head into my shoulders, but ripped my fingers down a dozen prickly links, tearing tiny pieces of skin from my all too small hands.

I cried no doubt. I rolled on the ground and whimpered to mommy and pouted for as long as I felt the need. Luckily I was alone so I had no audience who would certainly remember the incident and use it to my humiliation many decades in the future.

But I've never forgotten the time I nearly touched the clouds, when but for a minor mathematical error on my part, I very well may have been the first kid on my block to make a full circle on a park board swing set.

Many years later when I'd learned to fly, I stuck my hand out the window of my small plane while passing through the bottom of a cumulous cloud; just to finish what I'd started.

Name Changes Imminent

The triplets hated being alphabetically first, particularly in school. Each year they hoped an Anderson or Ackman would join their class, but to no avail. The Anyold boys were triply doomed to be the talk of home room as attendance was called… "Anyold, Tom? Dick? and Harry?"

Past Presently

There was a time when I was thin
when eating wasn't such a sin
and exercise was painless although sweaty and a bore
when I had scads of yellow hair
and piles of pocket change to spare
when riding was less transport than a reason to explore

Where did it go, my squandered youth
my gentle tone, my cosmic truth
what happened to the me that I would like to think exists
as now I'm just a lump of lard
more motley kook than avant garde
I want my past self presently, the one with fewer twists

You can't go back the sages say
yet I might relish far less gray
and what I'd do for inches off my waistline would amaze
I'm tired of disease du jour
I need some haute in my couture
this growing old is such manure, I pray it's just a phase

A Ponderous Box

Normally I wouldn't pay a breath of attention to a child. I'm of the W.C. Fields school of young progeny appreciation; hopefully not seen, neither heard. But I couldn't help but notice the apprehension clouding the face of a nearby tenish year old girl. She seemed alone; at least my scanning the 32 unfilled bus depot seats within our proximity provided no clue as to who might be her guardian. That in itself made me nervous for her, and I decided to at least keep her within my sightline until she appeared safe. But what had caught my eye and continued to make me curious was her cradling a small object in her hands as if it were a baby bird having fallen from a nest. I struggled to see what it was that she was enamored by, without of course making it obvious I was looking at her at all lest some hothead vigilante get the wrong idea.

Finally I caught a glimpse of her prize; a matchbox sized ceramic container, a rosemaled, alabaster coffer, no doubt containing some picture, coin or other keepsake of great worth.

You'd think once I'd seen the item my curiosity would have been sated, but alas, I soon became obsessed with the object and its possible contents. (Sitting alone in a small town bus terminal for hours, waiting on the last of two daily coaches tends to make one insane with latent nosiness, waiting for any trigger with which to set it into meddlesome motion.

"Young lady" I abruptly mumbled; "might I ask what it is that you're holding? It seems so precious to you."

Without so much as looking up she said "It's my box of flaws! And my mom says I need it with me at all times."

My mind began chewing that answer immediately, like a raccoon with a discarded fast food bag. "A box of flaws." How cute if it were meant to relieve the child of the self-made guilt that surrounds the discovery of imperfection; a little box in which to store flaws so that the girl would never be burdened by them.

Or, how loutish of a parent to make issue of a child's shortcomings; to force the youngster to carry with them a constant reminder of their failing to meet the parent's expectations. A box of flaws indeed!

Yet either way it was heartwarming to me, endearing almost, that one so young could be moved by symbolism so simple, and yet so profound. One's flaws are ponderous things, no matter a person's inclination to either obsess their importance or forgive oneself their existence. And to have someone so young believe that she might store them in a tiny box to be held in her tiny hand, is a testament to the power of myth.

As I calculated the probabilities of flaws as saint or demon, hesitant to ask for resolution to my query as I was a stranger and children should never speak to me and mine, the girl sat, fluffed out her dress so as to make a lap and then sat the box into the center of the smoothed fabric. With one hand she held the ceramic tightly, and with the other she began to extrude a long piece of string from its interior. Once she'd pulled nearly a foot long strand, she jerked her hand away from her waist as if bitten by a spider, snapping off a healthy length of the material.

Then, as a smile slowly crept across my face, the angel twirled the ends of the string 'round her index fingers and slid the material between her slightly bucked front teeth.

"Floss" I said with a chuckle. "A box of floss."

It's good I'm not a parent, I thought. I have no ear for childese.

Small Talk

For Tom, the time between high school and college was his brandy summer; the culmination of a perfect aging process, expensive yet attainable, smooth, golden, to be sipped not merely swallowed. It was 3 months of heaven, a savory, guilty pleasure that capped fiercely long days of freedomless conformity, and welcomed the new paradigm of constant, self-fulfilling choice.

For Gwen, the time between high school and college was her brandy summer; overpowering, unreasonable, with a penchant to burst into all-consuming fire if exposed to the slightest lick of open flame. It was three months of hell, a rancid vinaigrette poured with malice past tender lips without a moment's sensitivity.

Tom and Gwen decided to try another topic, lest their blind date deteriorate into shouting and hurled insults.

Ron Runeborg

The Jack and Jill Chronicles
"Purity Pledge"

Jack and Jill
went up the hill
to fetch a pail of water

Jill had just turned eighteen and was simply brimming with pent up hormonal stuff. She watched intently as Jack's square hips swayed side to side as he lugged the heavy pail up Horner's Hill, his daddy's own piece of God's country. She caught her breath on the sight of his bulging biceps as he switched the bucket from one hand to another, and when they'd reached the top of the rise she could stand it no longer. She pushed Jack backward into the apple tree that stood watch over Hilltown and said to him in as sultry a tone as she could wrangle…

"I gotta have your hot steamy sex right now Jack, don't make me wait a minute longer or I'll have to kill myself. Kiss me, kiss me right this minute you hunk of pail carryin man!"

But Jack pulled away, shyly.

"Gosh sakes Jill, you know I can't do that" he sputtered. "Why, you of all people know that I've taken the pledge!"

"What pledge is that my love" Jill said as she again tried to co-mingle their two bodies into one.

"Why" (it annoyed Jill that Jack started most of his sentences with the word 'why', but at that moment she was so worked up she let even that pass) "Why, the Jonas Brothers pledge dearest! You know, the purity pledge!"

"Oh, screw the Jonas Brothers Jack, just do it! Do it now!!!"

"Why Jill," he answered, "I just can't. The Jonas Brothers are the best role models in all the world and if they say they're saving themselves for marriage, then I should do the same!"

"Fuckity fuck fuck fuck" screamed Jill, knowing that Jack's mind was made up and that she'd need to go without, at least for the hour that it'd take to collect the water and drop it off at the Horner house when she then could run through town and find the first real man she could see and drag him into the bushes.

Then she did what any Hilltop High School gymnastics champion might do if overwhelmed by a nearly quarter century of building sexual tension… she began to practice her floor exercise in preparation for the big meet on Saturday.

"Get the water your own damn self" she said as she completed a twirling cartwheel and somersault combination. But then as Jack filled the bucket and walked back toward the crest for the journey downward, she thought to one last time try and convince him of his error.

"Look Jack" she shouted, "your favorite routine!" Jill ran three steps and then began to flip forward and back, dancing and doing the splits, showing her perky breasts and thick athletic legs to their best advantage. But Jack was having none of it. He turned away, in spite of his tongue's sudden swelling and the sweat beginning to bead on his forehead. A promise was a promise, and he would be pure no matter what. He turned away and faced toward the parking lot far below.

As Jill attempted her final move, a triple back flip with two and a half twists, she knew she would come quite close to her soon to be ex lover's head, and while she knew what might happen if she didn't reign herself in, she completed the maneuver with a swift kick to the jerk's back, sending him sprawling down the hill and off the retaining wall that separated the nice soft grass from the hard as steel tar. Jill, oblivious to the damage she'd caused, continued down the hill doing cartwheels and pirouettes, or as the newspaper might have put it in the headline the next day…

Jack fell down
and broke his crown
and Jill came tumbling after.

But, of course, the paper never did print that header, because Jack suffered a great deal of neurological damage in the fall once he'd cracked his head open on the tarmac, and there he lost both his ability to speak, and his penmanship, so he could never tell the truth; that Jill had, in an abandoned rage, tried to kill him for not breaking his word to the Jonas Brothers.

Jill ended up marrying Billy Crackhead, the first real man she'd run into after Jack had been carted off to the hospital. He'd made no such promise. He was as pure as soot.

A Balloon Frog's Magic Carpet Ride

I'd never had "franked mushrooms" before, so as you can imagine I was ill prepared for the trip that was to follow. Sure, I'd eaten ordinary magic mushrooms; whole, powdered, skewered on a stick and toasted over an open fire and even stuffed with crabmeat and goat cheese. But never ground and stuffed into sausage skins. Frank and I settled in for a light hallucinogenic carpet ride, preparing the proper snacks, candles and black light posters for early take off. Then we ate.

Yes, they were delicious, grilled and sliced on the bias served with eggs Florentine and a dab of wild rice with baby peas and wild ginger; but there must be something about the grinding that puts the magic into the bloodstream faster than any other narcotic transportation system!

I first recognized I was high when I began to cannon giggle. "HA!" I said from the bottom of my diaphragm. "HA!" After each Ha was delivered I swiveled my head as if my neck were a gun mount and my mouth, a 50 mm barrel. "HA, HA!" I shot across the room at Fred who was suffering his own trip malfunctions, trying to emulate a worm in the form of a tree. He looked a bit like the girls who sang "Walk like an Egyptian" on videotape, squirming with his prayer folded hands over his head.

"HA" I blasted Fred right in the trunk, after which he gave me that hard smile; the one that the brain says to do in order to convince those around you that you are indeed having a great time and are not at all paranoid about losing your marbles or being dragged off to jail, while your body refuses to cooperate because it's busy being paranoid about how weird it feels and is angry that you did this to yourself, so you work and work and work at it until at last the corners of your lips raise just the tiniest amount and you turn to your friends and show them that yes, the fact that you can hard smile shows you are tripping and loving it!

Suddenly, I felt like a balloon frog in a zebra house! Zebras were stomping around making zebrazy noises and dropping clumpy zebra packages! I was teeny! I was terrified! If one stepped on me I'd pop for sure, and if I was smothered by zebra stuff... I'd be the laughing stock of the Mushroom Forest! Luckily, moments before an ill aimed package splatted on my froggy head, a falling leaf bunny floated to my rescue, scooping me up and carrying me to the sloped cow glade; where every cow stands at a slope so as to better see who's milking them.

I decided that I'd better hop off to a frilly whereabouts before another blatant impossibility presented itself. I waved deeply to the leaf bunny and immediately ran for the hills; at least as well as a balloon frog can run!

A voice called to me from somewhere in the murky, frosted sinkhole of a sky. "Sir" it said, "You must re-don your pants and leave the frozen foods cooler at once!"

BAM! The reality of the situation struck me between the eyes! I wasn't a balloon frog at all! I was a generic microwave snack, devoid of any nutritional value! I curled in the cold, gripping my toes with my hands, becoming the pound cake ring I'd always wanted to be. Then, the closing of a blinding electrified space door ejected my hopes into the great outerness of nothingness, canceling the black streak I'd left on the Book of

Great Men and setting fire to my bird child and the wave battery that

powered it. Like any dog in a fish tank, I was mortified!

Doctor, the patient is mumbling something about puppy chow and slippery ships. Are you sure I should leave him alone without first strapping him to his bed? Yes, doctor… I see… occasional lucidity… 24 hours… certainly, I'll watch for it. Have a nice father's day. See you tomorrow.

Old Friend Before His Time

Fifty pounds overweight yet gaunt
face drawn, eyes hollow, red rimmed
hair greasy, matted; shirt stained, shoes colorless
twenty years of twelve steps, now eleven shy
a lifetime of knowledge, skill, confidence
left to rot while in service one last year
or ten
another Samaritan consumed by homeless men
their never-ending needs a vacuum
sucking the life from those that will
until they can't
until they've passed through the gates
from living to existing to begging for a way out
another man who believed he could walk among the dead
and not become one

Ron Runeborg

Moon's Bright Idea
(A New Age Fairy Tale)

Once upon a time, the Moon was in a lather. It had been thinking quite deeply (for a lifeless rock) and had found itself stymied as to its own identity. So, it called for its friends to come sit nearby and help with its ponderings.

"Cow" it said with all due respect, "Now I know I'm the Moon, but that's just a name, you know? I must have some importance to me that transcends a silly moniker! *Moon Schmoon*, I want to know just who I am beyond the letters printed on space maps! Got any ideas?"

Cow thought for a very long time, which annoyed Moon greatly. "Well, I see you as the great hurdle!" Cow exclaimed. "You are the reason I jump! And **that** is very important indeed!"

"A HURDLE!" Moon was even more annoyed, if one can be more annoyed than one gets while waiting for a cow to speak. "A hurdle is 'in the way'! A hurdle is 'something to overcome'! I don't want to be a hurdle!"

"Well", said Cow reluctantly; "You are my *favorite* hurdle, if that helps any."

"**CAT!** Put down that fiddle and answer me!" shouted Moon. Who am I... exactly!"

Without hesitation, Cat played a little ditty and sang "You are whatever a moon has always meant, of course, of course, the moon has meant!"

Moon shook its craters. "Out of the catnip, Cat! How many times do I need to warn you!"

Suddenly, Moon noticed Dish and Spoon running past. With one shot of a well-placed beam it stopped them in their tracks.

"Please, Moon" Dish squealed, "We've heard you and have come to the same conclusion. You are the light by which we run! Now may we please run on and fulfill our destiny?"

Moon withdrew its beam and sighed heavily; about a moon's worth. "Well, that's not so bad, I could ponder that some. I am the light by which you run. I kind of like that."

Dog held up one paw. He fancied himself a bit of a poet and thought to curry favor with his nighttime garbage hunt searchlight.

"Yes, little Dog" Moon said, "Do you have a better answer for me?"

"As a representative of all things nocturnal" Dog replied, "I would say you are the brilliance to which I am tethered."

"Brilliance" the Moon smirked. "I like it, go on, go on!"

"You are the creator of all dark shadow, the illuminator of stolen kisses, the sovereign of the tides and the ivory circle of the skies!"

Moon was suddenly excited. "Wait! Say that again" it demanded.

"You are the Crea…"

"No, not that" Moon interrupted; "The kisses thing!"

Dog cocked his head, as all dogs are known to do. It was his worst metaphor he'd thought. He hoped moon wasn't angry, or it might be a month of new moons for this dog. Tentatively he answered, "You are the illuminator of stolen kisses?"

"YES! THAT'S IT!" Moon shouted in glee! "From this moment forward you shall call me… **THE ILLUMINATOR!!!**"

Cow groaned. "I kinda liked hurdle better, Moon" she said. "I mean can you imagine… "and the Cow jumped over the… *say what?!?!!*"

"Shut up" Moon said angrily; "What do you know, you're a cow." Moon turned to the Little Dog. "Thanks so much my fuzzy friend" it said. "I shall light your way to the garbage cans of your choosing from now, until… well, until the cows come home!"

Cow groaned again. "Nice one Moon", she giggled. "Can I jump you now your Illuminatorious?"

"Jump away" Moon trilled, and the Little Dog laughed to see such a sight as the cow jumped over the ~~moon~~ err… Illuminator!

The Fine Line Between Life and Death

They call it black snow. When the winds are so strong that they tear off the ice cover that normally resides atop the winter North Dakota prairie and scoop topsoil into the stratosphere where it shares the sky with snowflakes, turning the horizon to a dark brown. That morning the world was covered in a layer of filthy white and steam was rising from anything that dared to move. It was six am when the phone rang; two hours before my normal wakey wakey and three hours before my shift was to start. The morning guy was on the line, trapped by an uncooperative vehicle, 15 miles from the radio station. As I was only a mile off, could I sub for him until he was able to find his way?

KDLM was a daytime station, off line during the wee hours. Someone had to open shop, and since the weather was dramatically bad and there would be tons of school closings and other information to dole out over the air, someone had to turn on the lights and get the ball rolling. I had a purpose in my saying yes, beyond the obvious "help a guy out". I was fairly newly married and in a hurry to set up our lives so we could start a family. Being a radio personality was my chosen path and I was scurrying down its twisted route as fast as humanly possible in order to make my way to a "major market" and some modicum of financial security. To that end I would do almost anything; twelve hour days, remote sales junkets in white guy hostile territory, wedding discos in the station's name. I'd already written and voiced more and better commercials, ran longer and more complex shows, interpreted reams of incoherent news and created more enjoyable musical excursions than anyone I worked with, probably than anyone that had ever worked at the bodunk media outlet. While I had zero desire to get out of bed before dawn, showing loyalty in impossible circumstances would be a perfect piece to the resume puzzle. I said yes, in spite of knowing the forecast was for subzero temps and snow blinding flurries.

It might have occurred to me that the morning guy had a new car and I, a beat up 15 year old station wagon, before I'd agreed. Had it, I might have thought to try and start my own car before jumping down the ice hole. But I showered and dressed, oblivious to the obvious. I too, would be mechanically immobile, as were most of the residents of the county I'd guess.

Being a "man of your word" has its up and down sides. This was a downer to be sure. I couldn't call the guy back and beg off my chore. I could, within my moral code, call the afternoon jock and try and sucker him into the job. But I'm just not cruel enough for that. I had to walk, there was no other real choice. It was at least a straight line and doubtful that I would get all the way there without some adventurous spirit coming upon me in their nicely warmed and graciously appointed automobile, begging for a chance to play the good Samaritan by taking a local celebrity to work.

There's no way to dress for 40 below zero, unless you're an Antarctic explorer and your bank account is filled with oodles of grant monies. When one buys outdoor gear with which to live in the tundra, one spends what one can afford to suit the average mean temperature, not the worst case scenario. Regardless, unless you have a dozen coats, one for each ten degree change, you're either over or under dressed. In this case it was not a problem. What I could afford was nothing really, hence the need to rapidly rise to the top of my profession. I slipped on my 15 below parka and my gloves with the fingers cut off them, my stylish wonder fabric headband and my tennis shoes and ever popular clipable rubber boots, and stepped outside for the long trudge.

You'd think I would have noticed the house creaking and leaning against the insistence of a frigid gale before I'd opened the door. But alas, I am a man of focus, and so focused was I on simply staying upright and conscious that I'd missed the vinyl siding rattling and the red osier dogwood branches lashing at my windows. I could see the station from the end of my driveway, on any other day. But this morning all I could see was a huge piece of off white vellum stretching from sky to earth, west to east. And so I hunkered, as men of the north are wont to do, and let gravity pull me toward my goal.

The first few hundred yards were tolerable as there were houses between the hurricane and I; but soon I was in the no man's land that stretched from town to the out of town property on which our radio hovel stood. Farm fields stretched from here to damn near the Rockies of Montana, and the wind could only pick up speed on such a pancake expanse. When one hunkers, one leans forward slightly, pulling one's shoulders together and tightening one's grip on the nothingness between one's fingers. Within a few feet I was hunkering as if I were a medicine ball, wanting only to roll downhill at the urging of natural phenomena. Being a "manliest of men" man, I had never owned an actual HAT in the true meaning of the word. I was a Swede by heritage, and quite proud of my immunity to frostbite. It was in fact unusual that I would succumb to even wearing an earmuff as protection of any sort upon one's head was forbidden by the "manliest of men code". Luckily, I had shucked that certain portion of my rulebook for this particular journey or I can guarantee I would be pictured today earless, with only duct tape to hold my fashionable sunglasses to my head. I don't believe I truly crawled the last half mile, but I know for a fact I'd have liked to, as the closer I would have been to the ground the less I would have had to keep myself from becoming airborne.

I've never been more grateful than I was at the moment I touched the handle of the door to my workplace. My lips were unmoving or I'd have cried out in joy. My eyes were watering and freezing so fast I could barely see the knob itself, but eventually I was able to gain purchase and pull myself indoors. Not that it mattered all that much. My breath inside was a solid; at least outdoors the wind was blowing so hard I couldn't witness the pain in my huffs and puffs.

It's a funny thing about propane. It's a liquid that turns gaseous, or something of the sort; only it seems there's a certain temperature at which it refuses to gasify. We'd reached that temperature; 40 below zero as I understand it, plus one. It was single digits inside the station, and there was nothing I could do but whine. Luckily, electricity doesn't freeze, or it might have. I powered up the transmitters and stepped into the control room to "flame on" the tools of my trade. The console lit, as well as the assorted tape decks and cart machines, but the turntables were a bit reluctant to turn. It took them somewhere near three minutes to get to full speed, as they spin on bearings smothered in grease; grease that was likely the consistency of moderately melted granite at that moment. I had to find a source of heat before I signed on. All there was beyond the transmitters themselves was the station coffee pot. Now why, in Swede territory, there was only one coffee pot in a building serving some dozen employees was beyond me. I could drink a pot by myself in one shift, on a hot summer's day no less. But, there it was and would have to do. I wired it up in front of the console and set its hot plate to cooking so at least I'd be able to bring my fingers from blue to bright red in case I actually needed to use them for anything.

The teletype was howling, the news was never ending, the phone was ringing off the hook. I signed on, said my hellos and flipped on Gordon Lightfoot's "Canadian Railroad Trilogy"; the only seven minute song in residence, generally reserved for bathroom breaks for solitary disk jockeys. It would take me a few minutes to collate all the information I'd been swamped by and as the turntables needed to be left running and every piece of music "slip cued" into play mode, I was forced to pile up all the longest songs in my recollection so as to have time to think about our collective predicament; and to smoke enough cigarettes between each delivery to warm at least my insides.

It was hours before anyone else showed up, and those were office people. I was on the board for the entire morning, in my coat, rubbing my hands over the coffee pot and muttering "uffda" as often as my lips would move. I gave at least a hundred school closings, the hog futures and the tennis scores, though Martina Navratilova was the only one winning in those days so who really cared anyway. I never played a song that timed out to less than 4 minutes, and played every commercial in the rack, whether it was on the traffic sheet or no, as all I had to do to accomplish that was load the cart and press a button and the friction created by the little piece of magnetic tape running across the machine's play head created a little heat I could absorb... or at least that's the lie I told myself.

Eventually, it warmed to somewhere above the 40 below mark and a local repairman had been called to set the furnace to a-blazing. I was relieved and was offered a ride home before the building had even warmed to polar bear status. I accepted but had them drop me at a local eatery a block from my house. I figured if I could walk a mile across Pluto, I could do a block on the polar ice cap, and I wanted some sort of prize for my courage and integrity. It might have been sex, or gold, or a promotion, or even worldwide acclaim, but crispy hash browns and over easy eggs would have to do.

I marvel at the fact I survived that morning. In whiteout, I easily could have gotten lost and wandered off to an early grave. It turned out that at its peak the wind-chill was 80 below, a record for that part of the country, and cold enough to have ripped 6 layers of skin off my bare face, not to mention my balding head. It's an example of the fine line between brave and stupid, honorable and irresponsible, the wisdom of time in grade and the presumed immortality of youth. I'm afraid to say I'm likely no wiser now 30 years later. I may whine a lot more before setting out, but I'd still take the walk... because it's what I promised to do. But then, being a little twisted makes for good storytelling experience, so at least there's a reasonable trade off.

The Lady Forkinbaby

"I realize it's your brother's friend and I should be nice to her, but for God's sake, it's a black spray painted naked doll with a fork sticking out of its belly! I don't really have to compliment it do I?"

Marie frowned, speaking a hundred pages of the 'wife's book of proper etiquette' with a twist of her lip. "Just do it" she added with a raised eyebrow.

I had few options. I could lie and destroy my self-image, or I could be honest and suffer the wrath of the assembled freshmen artsy-fartsies, most of which were now high on boilermakers made with ouzo. I decided to be clever, and try to use an "old school" phrase for honesty, hoping to have it received in a "new school" way, for the win.

"Fine Shit" I said as I smiled and pointed at her ridiculous excuse of an artistic masterpiece. "Hey, thanks Dude" goth-girl said grinning as her head pounded from shoulder to shoulder in some sort of satanically induced rhythm.

"Yup, some great shit" I repeated, visualizing her next work being a black spray painted pile of horse manure topped by a cherry. I moved on. I had more shit to appreciate.

Ron Runeborg

The Local Spooks

My first wife is long gone (not from the earth, from my sight if you will), but she did leave me with a few stories to tell. I used to recite them in a true but crass way, bitterness being the cruel master that it is. Now I try and avoid the guillotine and just go for the cheese. I know… but it makes sense to me…

We'd just been married and had rented an apartment. It was an old manse; a two story, late 19th century Victorian that had been turned into a duplex. We were on the first floor and no one had rented the upper at the time, or the attic which was livable.

We decorated in true hippy style, painting ceilings blue, walls red and trim white. "Gaudy patriotic" I'd call it. ("Shock value" if I were being honest) Our quarters were the old living-dining rooms plus kitchen and crappy little add on bath. But it was cool, full of old woodwork including a ceramic tiled fireplace and a beaded wooden room separator.

The living room had been built with a double pocket door in the center of the inside wall, now removed and replaced by sheetrock. This hid the original bedroom, which had then been made into a storage locker for yet another renter. To me, staring and pondering as I'm wont to do, it seemed a big picture frame with a blank wall inside, just screaming for objects d' art. Think of the time if you're able. I might have used fluorescent posters and black lights, or perhaps shelving covered in lava lamps of various sizes. Instead I bought black mirror and deep red carpet tiles from Sears and made myself a vertical, ivory reflecting pool surrounded by a rim of red shag umm... grass. In the words of the day it was way cool dude.

We slept in the dining room on a queen sized mattress and box on the floor. It was here the story begins.

I'd been driving cab that night and had come home at 3am expecting to find my honey asleep. All the lights were on; an odd sight. I went inside being as cautious as I was able considering I'd worked 12 hours and was now exhausted. Anita screamed, loud and long.

She scared the crap out of me. There she was sitting in the center of the bed, deluxe 14 inch long chef knife in hand and rocking her head around like a puppet looking for applause. We'd just seen the Exorcist that week and pea soup was on my mind. I stared at her for a minute hoping she wouldn't twist her head all the way around.

I finally got her calmed down enough to talk and she told me a little story.

The bed looked out into the living room where the black hole wall lived. My cowboy boots had been standing, facing that mirror for a day or two. She wasn't sure, maybe she was dreaming, but she swore she'd woken and had looked into that room where a man was standing in my boots facing the "wall". Of course she assumed it was moi. Then he turned toward her, started a slow walk to her side and spoke.

She didn't know what to do so she listened and swallowed her screams. He told her a story about having built the house we were in. His wife, an invalid lived upstairs, hence the duplicated bedrooms and baths on both floors. She wanted to have the view from the second floor and as she was in a wheelchair, getting up and down the two level stair was impossible.

Long story short, this woman fell down the stairs one day and died on the landing that was just outside our front door. She'd lost an earring, one of a set. He had no idea where but he knew where the other was…a hidden compartment in the built in buffet across from our bed.

Don't ask why but he wanted my wife to have the jewelry; so she says, dream that it was. Then, she has no idea what happened. She woke up and was scared shitless by the sound of her own breathing. She ran to the kitchen, grabbed a knife and sat in the center of the bed pressed against the wall, waiting for Satan to make a house call. I showed up instead.

I finally convinced her it was just a dream and got her to sleep, not because I knew what to think but because I was exhausted and to stay awake any longer would give me a migraine. I thought about investigating the buffet, but I really didn't want to find this thing. So I slept as well.

The next day though, feeling a lot more confident in the sunlight, I searched for this hidden compartment. Lo and behold I found it; and damn if there wasn't an earring in it along with some other junk; a triangular Masonic looking metal plate earring with a teardrop pearl hanging.

Ok, now I was getting the heebie jeebies. I didn't want to tell my wife. We needed one of us to be sane and it wasn't going to be me at this point.

I went to the foyer and looked around. It was all too obvious. There was a cold air register on the floor right at the foot of the stairs; A large one with a wooden grate. So ok, if I reach into it what are the odds some hand will grab mine and try to pull me into the aluminum shaft? I thought about it. I couldn't help it. It's my way.

Like a kid taking his first bite of limburger I kinda held my nose, closed my eyes and reached down into the huge dust ball that 80 years of neglect had built. Hmmm, pencil, some dining utensil…I pulled them and the life-sized dust bunny out of the hole, heart pounding a thousand beats a minute.

As I pulled the poof out of the vent I heard a little metal on metal scrape. I waited for the screams of a zombie; but none came. I leaned over and looked down, now holding a flashlight to light the pit. There….it was a small piece of metal glinting. FUCK! It was a triangular Masonic looking metal plate earring with a teardrop pearl hanging.

I damn near had my first heart attack 20 years ahead of schedule. I'm shivering now and looking about just thinking about it. Never write a ghost story at 3am.

We moved as soon as we were able, not an easy task for a young cab driver/waitress couple.

But….we were…..motivated. I think she still has the earrings. Maybe they house her demons. I can only hope she has them safely locked up and ready for deposit in the nearest volcano.

Ron Runeborg

Off Track Vetting

"Yes I'm coming! As soon as I find my keys!"

I wonder where they might have gone. I was sure they were right here on my desk. It's so frustrating. I have to believe people move things on me just to test me or something. Oh I don't know, maybe I'm just being forgetful. I suppose I should sit a moment and think about it, I'm sure it'll come to me. They could still be in my other pants pockets I guess; maybe the jeans with the rip in the right knee, or is it the left. No wait, I think I was wearing shorts earlier, or was I. Hmmm. Maybe in my coat pocket. Sure that's it, the coat.

There she is yelling to me again. I wish I knew who this woman was, she tramps around my house like she owns it, always asking me questions. "What do you want for breakfast" she asks, like I can't fix my own. "Put some socks on", "did you brush your teeth?" "Stay close" she says, as if I'd wander off, as if I'm a child. Hurry this and hurry that. I wonder "what's her hurry, there's plenty of time in a day".

Wait a second, I remember now. She was yelling at me earlier, in the back yard, scooting me off the lawn like I was some goose pooping in her grass, whispering at me to put some clothes on if I wanted to be outside. No one could see me for God's sake, there are shrubs for that around the patio and the people in the house behind us weren't home, or at least weren't peering out their windows while I was peering toward them. So what does it matter what I wear, as if I can't be casual on my own property.

Well that cracks it. If I was outside and undressed, it must have been warm since I'm no fool after all; so obviously the keys aren't in my coat. It's summer silly. Maybe the shorts after all. I wonder where they are. I suppose they're upstairs in the dirty clothes hamper where they always are, where I always find them even though I've told my wife I need them so please wash them once in a while so I have them handy when I need to go out and enjoy the sunshine.

"Yes dear, I'm coming! Really! I just have to find my keys!"

I called her dear. There must be a reason; I'm not one to call strangers dear after all. Oh, oh, OH! Linda! My wife! That's who's been yelling at me to hurry up! Of course you moron! Who else would it be! Yes, Linda. She must want to go somewhere and needs me to drive her. If only I could find my damned keys. They must be around here somewhere. I wonder if they're in my coat pocket. Wait; wasn't that...

I wonder if I should just tell her I can't find my keys. I don't really want to disappoint her again. I'm such a disappointment lately. I should tell her I suppose, so she can make other plans or find her own ride to wherever she's going. Where's she going I wonder. Maybe she told me already. I could ask, but she might worry that I didn't know; she seems to worry a lot lately ...

Ron Runeborg

Serious Takes a Beating

One doesn't have a sense of humor. It has you ....**Larry Gelbart**

Fear pounded his gavel three times and called out, "Intellect, if you would bring the meeting to order please; some of us have to get back to work before the host awakens."

"Alright people let's get to it." Intellect stood so that he might look down on the others; an annoying trait to those who could recognize an act of superiority in action. "Let the fifty first annual meeting of the Ronsense Society begin! Madame Secretary, please interview each member in order to discern our host's current status."

Touch nodded and walked toward the chalkboard, her overstated, hip heavy gait eliciting more than one whispered mansensical comment.

"Taste! You stop that sexist blather right now or I'll flatten your nodes!" Touch said as she whipped around and pointed her digit directly into the tongue of the most egregious offender.

"No harm meant miss" Taste replied with a smarmy chuckle; "I was just admiring your umm, circulation."

Intellect dramatically sighed as if a steam locomotive at a water tank. "Geez I hate when braniac does that" Hearing whined to Sight; "He's supposed to be the smart one here, why can't he just run these damn meetings rather than pretend like he's above it all."

"Enough with the infighting children" Insight said; "We have a serious problem and if we don't solve it together, we could all be in danger."

"Well said Six!" Intellect applauded his roommate, the sixth sense; "the host has been morose for some time now and could possibly be headed for suicide, or worse, public drunkenness. We need to rectify his mood or suffer the consequences associated with late night vomiting and uncontrollable weeping."

"Man I get bloodshot just thinkin about it" said Sight; to which Taste laughed aloud... "Bloodshot!" he said cynically; "Spend a night in my shoes at the foot of the porcelain god. Trust me eyeballs, Taste and vomit don't mix!"

Hearing began to sneeze as a flowery scent wafted into the room, the perfume carried by a soft breeze. In the doorway stood Smell, her little black nose bobbing up and down as her head turned this way and that, acknowledging her compatriots each in turn. "There's only one answer boys" she purred; "Humor will get him through this rough patch, you've got to appeal to his sense of Humor."

The group began to talk amongst themselves. "Yea, just where is Humor lately?" said one. "Humor schmoomer, what the hell's wrong with me?" said Taste; "Get the guy to buy a case of Hostess Twinkies and I'll change his mood for ya pronto!"

"No Twinkies!" shouted the custodial team Bloodstream and Bacterium. "Mood alteration by sugar high is inefficient and potentially dangerous, not to mention messy at a later date."

"Alright hold up now" Intellect said as he pounded his gavel for silence so as to shoosh the collected senses and assorted affectations. "Humor, what do you think; can you make him let go of Seriousness so you can squeeze into the psyche and give us all a rest?"

Humor set down his beer, pulled out his compact mirror and checked his makeup before speaking. "Do I have floppy orange clown shoes?"

"Yes" The crowd muttered.

"And orange curly hair and a red nose?"

Taste laughed and the crowd followed. "Why yes; you do!" The audience cheered as Humor rose to his floppy orange feet.

"Well, then stand back people, cuz Humor's gonna take control of this helpless host. I'm off to kick some Serious ass!"

And the crowd roared as the host giggled in his sleep....

Brainstorming

Ronald Jackson stepped through the double doors and into the Gitchegoomie conference room where an impatient collection of creative directors, writers and artists were awaiting him; their new client.

"Sorry I'm late," he said cheerily as he walked to the head of the table and gripped a leather chair back, leaning toward the gathered and slowly taking in each face one at a time.

Horrified and quite speechless, the elite of Mason-Williams Advertising stared at the new arrival; a tall, muscular man with an unusually elongated face framed by swept back, coal black hair. His ears seemed a little too pointed as did his teeth, which showed themselves as he smiled in greeting, his upper lip near folding onto itself, baring a set of unusually long, gleaming canines. But it was the still dripping mess covering the client's Italian suit that had the staff excessively worried. By the color of the stain on his white shirt the liquid had to be blood, but worse were the obvious bits and shards of flesh and bone stuck to clothing and hanging from his well-trimmed beard.

"I've met with your director and sorry to say we had a disagreement as to his creative proposal. He was very adamant yet, I just couldn't get my claws around the idea. Does someone else have a better concept? A show of hands?"

Ron Runeborg

A Spire for Bishop Clannad

Awash in the view of their great white cathedral
the vicar and minions were deeply distraught
One fine silken thread of their web of deception
had snagged on a sliver of freedom of thought

The weave, at a snail's pace, unraveled by inches
until there were only a few random strands
They'd claimed there were heretics working against them
that they'd not absconded with good King John's lands

Now most men would bow to the words of the clergy
If one said "I didn't" then surely "he'd not"
A few though were classified drunken transgressors
and one could trade whiskey for truth from a sot

So armed with a bottle and charm from my mother
I treated a friar to sips of good cheer
and whilst he was tipsy I questioned "his plumpness"
about missing monarchs and church held frontier

He yapped like a bloodhound of classified knowledge
The king was imprisoned by Bishop Clannad
"Keep secret" he told me "this sad state of reason;
the Bishop was said to be ordered by god!"

By its common name this was treason in earnest
a grasp for true power, a vein mortal sin
Once they'd been apprised of John's thoughts of conversion
the church dragged him off to their darkness within

Old Shorts and Poetree

I pondered the wisdom of trying a rescue
a mouse in a lion's den might have no chance
Yet though if I failed I would face a new gallows
'twas better to die than to live in a trance

So armed I made haste to the manse of a builder
where records were stored of the castle and yard
I searched through the drawings and found in the rubble
old cellars once used by the Church's home guard

I sketched a quick outline, a catacomb puzzle
and left to confer with a strong, fearless friend
Once he had subscribed to my haphazard notion
we found an old entrance and made to descend

……..

An hour of wading through cobwebs and spiders
an hour of sloshing through sewage I'd guess
our liege was discovered at last by good fortune
chained down to the floorboards in tortured distress

We soon were detected while quickly escaping
my friend carried John while I fought with the priests
My sword was a-dancing through clerical collars
as we made our charge through the pastoral beasts

Once he had recovered the King made a statement
a Dire Editorial, from the High Crown
The Bishop would hang from his white spire of treason
and then the cathedral would promptly burn down

Ron Runeborg

The True Connection Between Cracks and Mothers' Backs
From the pages of the Sugartown Star

Mary Jane Lumpette of 1122 Snickerdooley Boulevard, Sugartown, is resting comfortably after having emergency surgery to repair a suddenly and quite mysteriously broken back. Her son, Clarence Lumpette, (aka Lumpy Lump) is being held for questioning as regards the alleged "incident involving possible malicious intent."

Police chief Bruhaha would only say there is an investigation underway and that he could not comment further. The Sugartown Star however has discovered a witness to the perceived crime; one Bobby Ratchooer, best friend of young mister Lumpette. As Ratchooer recalls, it was just one of those things kids do for fun, and it seems to have gone horribly wrong.

"We were just playing around the high voltage lines you know? As kids will do!" said Bobby; "Up by the witch Mrs. Creepingsly's house."

The editors of the Sugartown Star hereby make clear that the use of the word "witch" is a direct quote from the witness and in no way represents the views of the newspaper or its sponsors.

"We were doing the normal stuff you know? Playing marbles and spinning tops and stuff. And all of a sudden this crack appeared in the sidewalk. It happened real slow like, ya know like a circus strongman was ripping a telephone book in half or something. We didn't even notice it was glowing and stuff until it was too late, all I could think of was that old chant 'step on a crack, break your mother's back' and so I sang it out loud and then Lumpy said 'Take this Mom!' real loud ya know like he really meant it? Then anyway, he jumped right on the crack and we heard this horrible scream at the exact same time coming from way down the hill by Lumpy's house so we just ran our butts off to get there cuz Lumpy thought his mom might have found his Playboys under his bed, but when we got there Mrs. Lumpy was screamin and cryin and stuff and yelling about how her back must be broken. So I ran and hid under my bed until you guys came over and my dad dragged me into the living room and told me to 'fess up' cuz he knew whatever it was, I musta done it!"

The sidewalk in question has been roped off by police as a possible crime scene, and National forensic scientists are at this moment searching for any evidence of linkage between the crack and Mrs. Lumpette's malady.

When asked if there was a definite correlation between the two, all Mr. Ratchooer could say is "Well duh!" That seems to be the prevalent opinion of the majority of adolescents interviewed this afternoon at the Sugartown Mall as well.

Emergency Medical Technician Steven Liplok said "we may find there is no connection at all; but in the meantime my advice is, don't be stepping on any cracks until we know for certain."

Ron Runeborg

The Dust of Little Stories

He'd been working on it his entire life; at least since the age of one or two. It started small at first. Tiny screws and tacks were found in various carpets. It's all one could expect a toddler to find after all. Then, smallish slabs of wood, mostly multi-ply but some hard and soft woods. By age six he'd formed the legs, by eight the first row of cubbies, by nine the next and so on until the cabinet stood 12 cubbies high and 36 across. The drawers were difficult, though had he not reached the age of eighteen they'd have been impossible. Curved metal handles, the type libraries use for their index files, those that index *fingers* might just fit horizontally below were added last, as they required a bit of cash as much as desire and a steady hand. Finally, the labels; each face of each drawer sporting glued and screwed plaques announcing the names of his emotions, one by one.

To the top left was Surprise, for example. It was high enough that no one could see what was actually in the drawer until one drew from it a vial of its contents; a clever enough symbolism on his part, but sadly the drawer had been empty for many years, and even the few surprises drawn from it to date had not been very surprising.

The center of the apothecary hutch was less artful, more pragmatic. There in one row left to right were Envy, Jealousy, Depression, Hate, Malice and so on; in another row were Rapture (nailed shut), Acceptance, Love, Complacency and the like.

Although it had taken the better part of thirty years to build the *émouvoir armoire*, the daunting task truly, was to attempt the filling of the drawers, so as to have an emotion ready when needed. Joy, for instance, was impossible to find. He'd thought to have stumbled across a vial of the substance early on, but discovered it was only a potent philter of happiness, thus the subsequent mixing of a dash of annoyance with a single thread of disappointment, the ingestion of which caused the aforementioned permanent closure of the rapture drawer.

By his 55th year he had sampled at least once, each of his drawers' substances (save that of joy), whether elixirs or distillates, effusions or suspensions, philters or simple dehydrated resins; but of many he was able to find only one dosage, and no amount of searching would bring him another. Optimism was one of these, as were anticipation, zest, eagerness… oh I could go on. It was not that he'd never tasted of each, nor that he simply didn't understand every possibility contained therein. They were only such rare commodities within the sphere of his influence, capturing them even the single time was a near magical feat, and lately he'd grown tired of the hunt.

On this particular day he waffled, reading through his labeling system as though he hadn't seen it a thousand times before.

"What shall I be today" he muttered. "Grouchy? Satisfied? Oh, there are a few vials of guilt if I want to go that way, though I was guilty just a few days ago, for what reason exactly I can't remember now. If only I had a drawer of Stymied, I could spend the day staring at the ceiling without having to choose. But, here we are there's really no choice, choose I must. Hmmm, Caring? Nah, tired of caring. Lust? Tempting, but no purpose really. Enthusiasm? Hell, I'm not even awake yet, and there's only a few left anyway; I may as well save them for someone's birthday party so I don't have to fake it."

In the end, he had whittled his choices down to two; contentment, and bitterness. There were a few small sacks of contentment left. He'd used up all his happiness and had been filching the stores of contentment and complacency as often as he could. Now those cubbies were nearly empty and the harvesting of said emotions had become far too dependent on the weather, not to mention the day of the week.

What he did have though, in droves, was bitterness. In fact, one entire vertical row of drawers was labeled bitterness, as he'd rustled up so much of it to begin with, and as everyone knows it is one of the most self-propagating emotions available, why he just didn't have space for all the bitterness at his command.

Bitterness or contentment; Bitterness or contentment. It was some time before he made his choice, but ever so slowly, so as to not chance spilling a single grain, he slid open the box of contentment and dissolved a single wax paper sleeve of the gray powder into a glass of water, downing it before he'd so much as stirred. It's not as if the bitterness would go away, there was plenty to be had and surely he would have his fill before the cabinet was emptied; but for this one day he decided to write a pleasant story, one that said little, but was contentment unto itself. For this was his purpose in life, to write little stories that might somehow recreate contentment, that he might restock his cabinet and spend a few more days within its embrace.

Are You a Man or a Moose?

Marie and I had only been dating a month when I proposed we take a motorcycle trip to Yellowstone by way of the Tetons. In this tale, a woman who had never ridden on two wheels before, agreed to a 4000 mile camping trip without a moment's hesitation. She was game, I'll have to give her that.

By the time we reached central Wyoming, she was a seasoned rider, as we had already faced off with death, and she'd found it oddly pleasurable. While attempting to descend from the crest of Tensleep canyon on a switchback road that was in the process of being rebuilt, we had been forced to travel too fast by an eighteen wheeler whose brakes had overheated while on our tail, and I'd had to lay the bike down in the gravel to keep from jetting off a 500 foot cliff. Once she'd gotten over the initial shock, and found all her limbs intact, she'd wanted hot sweaty sex as quickly as conditions allowed. I took note of her response to danger, and quashed my fear that she might find riding just too scary for her liking.

The town of Dubois lies 85 miles from Jackson Hole, our presumed destination of the day. Though I say presumed, in reality it was more necessity as there's nothing between the two towns but rock, freezing water and goats. It was late afternoon, the weather was looking dicey; even in August in high elevation there was always the chance of snow. I'd not anticipated the possibility so we were lacking the gear we'd need should an early storm whack us enroute. Luckily, Dubois has a cowboy clothing store, and we stopped off for long undies and woolen socks.

While exiting the store, she pointed to a small restaurant up the street, identified by a 30 foot tall blue moose standing in front of its windows. I was nervous about the sky, but figured we had the 20 minutes it'd take to satisfy her hunger, so we sauntered into "the Blue Moose" (wouldn't you know) and ordered burgers and fries. It was self-serve, probably a converted fast food joint, so we grabbed our plastic trays and headed off for the streetside booth where we might watch the traffic, and the all-important heavens.

Marie took a large bite of her burger, looked up toward me and snorted, nearly losing the bite in the process. I said gesundheit as any gentleman would, and she giggled. She struggled to swallow, and once completing her mission, broke into a grin, then a smile, then a chuckle and then a belly laugh. I had to wonder what my face must have been smeared with to cause her such pain. I have to admit for just one moment I thought she was laughing at me. It wasn't paranoia mind you, but we were still feeling each other out so to speak, and there was a lot of her brain I'd not yet been witness to.

She must have noticed me thinking too hard, as I'm wont to do, because she said "no, no; look behind you!"

I turned and looked. The highway was empty, the sky growing brownish, the parking lot cracked and sprouting grass blades a-plenty. "What the hell are you seeing that I'm not" I said.

"Look up" said she; "it's a he".

"Well of course it's a he" I answered before I turned my head again, "the antlers…"

Then I saw them. Blue testicles. Blue testicles the size of navigation channel buoys. Blue testicles that must have weighed 200 pounds apiece.

"Hole crap" I said, "that's a healthy moose!"

I had to think about the making of a genitally correct moose. When the store owner decided to create an eye-catching billboard that might draw people to notice the "good eats" sign on the Blue Moose café frontage, what was it that made him decide "let's make sure the animal has all its working parts." Why? Just in case it came to life one night and ran off? Like a blue chick moose would wander by and do that moose whistle thing and maybe his blue moose would get together with Ms. Blue Moose and make baby mooses and he could start a traveling circus act with the blue moose family?

Then it occurred to me that it might be something far more insidious. The owner was probably a man, though I'm only guessing that because in my mind I just can't see a woman saying "I think I'll start a restaurant in the tiniest town in Wyoming in the middle of nowhere and in front of the store I'll commission a sculpture of a giant anatomically complete blue moose!" Of course, I could be wrong, but that's how my mind was working at the time so humor me.

Now since it was a man, and men have a tendency to express themselves in ways that symbolize themselves, or at least their notions of themselves, and that usually means something phallic, like constantly swinging a baseball bat or making grunting noises to replicate huge, fierce grizzlies, why couldn't it be that the guy decided to build a giant symbolic replica of himself in the form of the king of the wilderness beasts!

What's stronger than a moose? What's more fearsome, more manly man-ly, more testosterony?

Well, then it would stand to reason that he would make sure the moose was well endowed, as he is, (even if he isn't; in fact, **more likely** even though he isn't) and then lookin' out his business' front windows every morning would be just like looking in the mirror, sort of, presuming the mirror was behind him and hung below his waistline.

Needless to say, I laughed out loud, thinking about this self-made man, self-making himself into a giant blue moose with giant blue testes. Luckily, Marie just assumed I was laughing at the same thing she was laughing at, and I never did have to explain to her that I was insane; until later, just before the divorce.

We left just as the sky grew thick, and black. Within a few miles it began to rain, that cold drizzle kind of rain that says "I could be snow but that would be too easy for you so I'll be below freezing temperature rain instead and soak you to the bone". (Rain is such an ass sometimes.)

Marie was a champ. She just snuggled in behind me and kept her whining to herself for the hour and a half ride in the dark and what turned into a good pour. I have no doubt I wouldn't have made it, save some afternoon sex behind a grove of young spruce, the giant cotton long undies that now soaked in all the water from within ten feet of me like a paper towel on steroids, and the vision of the restaurant owner, designing a thirty foot tall blue moose with giant balls, setting down his pencil and muttering "yup, don't let anyone tell ya Jim Bob Chokterwhump ain't a hell of a man!"

The Construct King

And so it came to pass once more,
that neither Queen nor paramour
would give the king a man child heir,
before he'd met his doom.
The council met and there decreed
a new king born of blessed seed
would take the throne of Faelish
on the day he'd breached the womb

'Twas never writ but understood
the stag of sacred Kingsheart Wood
must mate the high Drouess
within the circle of the Wych!

The child conceived would bear quite soon,
(half dozen brightenings of the moon)
delivered in a clover field,
on heath and willow switch.

And once young sir could heft a blade
the folk would march a fine parade
to crown the King their custom made
twixt predator and prey.

A King of all the land's Droui,
a King of common folk to be;
A King created by the stars,
and customs of the Fae.

Ron Runeborg

Repentant Transparency

When I was asked to accept management duties within a corporation, my acceptance meant something beyond the obvious responsibility; I would have to play the game. Oh, not for my own boss as he was not only comfortable with my slovenly, pony-tailed appearance but thought it made me look as if someone who knew his craft, but for his superiors, so as to keep his reflection as crisp and clean as possible.

It was a great deal of money I was given to step into the hot box, so I spent it on the appropriate accoutrement. Of course, my size was an issue as I have never been "average" and have always struggled to find wearable wrappings. So against my deep set hippy grain I procured the services of a suit tailor and a custom shirt maker.

Now there were things I wouldn't do, such as whack my longish hair into a crew, and wear wing tip shoes; but I did begin to circle my rear locks with various bands, and I bought a few new pair of damned expensive cowboy boots, so I might stay in Dude mode yet sport a shine-able foundation.

My wife of the moment was all in favor of the change, being a newly christened social climber married to a common slug, and I was happy to allow her smugness as when momma ain't happy, ain't nobody happy, and since I was forced to do it anyway, why not intimate it was all for her.

I was actually quite pleased with the outcome for a time, thinking myself moderately dapper and a peer to the hogs at the trough of commerce. In fact, I nearly came to enjoy it, the jewelry and Egyptian cotton, the deerskin leathers and dinners by candlelight. And then the inevitable happened.

During a presentation to an "uplander", I was in the midst of explaining the enormous return from my suggested infinitesimal purchase when the manager my boss and I were speaking to, saw right through all the gold and Italian silks and saw me for the no class, reluctantly compromising biker I am. Yes, he zinged me, a few times in fact, intimating his belief that I surely was a penitentiary inmate in my recent past. Why? For fun I have to guess, simply to call me out, to assure me that he wasn't fooled and to make certain that I understood that I was not and never would be his peer, or anything of the sort.

I didn't hit him. Not really. Not so he might have noticed. In my mind I did, over and over and over and over. But again, the guy who'd given me the opportunity to pretend to be a corporate middle manager didn't deserve the fallout that would come if I'd broken every facial bone beneath the skin of the smarmy creep that would be his immediate superior.

I did the next best thing. I hung up the suits, stowed the shirts and ties and boxed up the accessories. Then, I reacquainted myself with myself, and emblazoned a platitude across my forehead that read, "Warning, Leopard Spots Unchangeable. Do not Attempt Modification or Risk Violence." The wife of the moment was not pleased, but had she been, she wouldn't have been the wife of the moment, now would she?

Ron Runeborg

Mama Sang Base

I remember it as if it were yesterday; like the moment I first saw Regan in "The Exorcist" turn her head all the way around and shoot fake vomit across the room, or when I saw one of the "13 ghosts" glide across the stage in "Black and White Cinematic Illusion-O!".

I was driving my mother to some event downtown when on the radio, the dj started talking about some survey noting the most unusual places people had experienced sex.

"*Daddy and I did it in a rocking chair once.*"

I nearly screamed, then, choked back the vomit. The thought of my parents having sex organs at all, much less having sex, much less adventurous sex... it almost made me blind.

"*Yea, like I wanted to know that*" I said, my voice solid and deep despite my insides being disgruntled and quivery.

"*I was talking to the radio*" she said as if that were any better line than the one I'd use when caught shoplifting; "*honest, I don't know how it got there!*"

"*You're going to hell you know*" I said.

"*Oh relax*" she said; "*parents are human too.*"

It had never occurred to me. I still think she was exaggerating. Not about the sex I'm sorry to say. Just about the parents being human thing...

The Dragon Whisperer

Poor Jason had been left by the side of the road, in a basket the size of a hay wagon. While in some countries he might have been seen as a blessing, a gift of the gods, the "appointed one", here in Tolkeinesque Englandish he was a freak, a curse, a mother's worst nightmare.

There was no record of any albino dragon having lived in the world, and the science of history was at least a thousand years old. Yet here was a baby albino dragon, abandoned and hungry, and slightly confused.

"Mommy?"

"No, I'm not your mommy, child" Brigitta replied as she and her sons Blinken and Nod hauled Jason into their own wagon; "but I will love you as a son."

As a founding member of the kingdom's oldest and smallest society "The Dragon Whisperers", Brigitta knew what would befall a dragon whelp left to the elements. Beyond the obvious, a rapid starvation, the hills were alive with predators. No, the animals would know not to approach a dragon, even a baby, even a "cursed" baby. It was the two legs, the human animals that endangered dragonkind, as they endangered the very planet they lived upon. The king would want the child's head, the hunters would kill it for its hide, the butchers for its meat, the physicians for its organs, the religious for its horns and teeth and the illusionists for its poison sacs, which when ground into a fine power could be set aflame creating huge puffs of smoke and temporary paralysis for any within range;

the perfect screen within which one might seem to maneuver time and space.

There were already too few dragons, and none so beautiful as this milky white specimen with its pink eyes and patterned scales.

The crone spoke softly to her charge as her wagon bucked through the moguls and ruts of King's Road. "Do you have a name my darling one?"

"Jason" he replied; "Mommy named me Jason. Where is my mommy?"

"I'm afraid dear Jason that your mommy has decided to allow me the honor of teaching you of the sublime wonders and treacherous snares of the world at large. I am sure she will come for you one day, far in the future, when her many pressing obligations have been met and she has all her time to spend loving you."

Jason seemed to be satisfied by Brigitta's answer. He sat very still for the next few minutes, staring off into the distance as if searching for a retreating pair of wings. Finally he turned, looked into the old woman's cobalt blue eyes and said…

"I'm hungry!"

Brigitta leaned toward the cart's driver and tapped her son on the shoulder.

"Watch for a wayward cow" she said; "baby needs a bite."

Fern of Little Cabbage Farm

Fern was more than a little annoyed. Her newly adopted son had rejected nearly every food she'd set before him. Happily, he hadn't thrown the dishes as her natural daughter had right from the start, and right through her teens. No, he just sat there playing with his fingers and humming songs of spiders and drainpipes.

He was an odd looking child for certain, but her husband Geoffrey had demanded she adopt a boy if her womb couldn't produce a natural son as he was getting on and would need a hand on the farm soon enough. And it seemed at that moment, the world had run out of adoptable male children. Jack was the only one left!

"Please Jack" she said, "eat your miniature cabbages! They're good for you!"

"Name not Jack" Jack said; "me gots no name! No need!"

"Alright sweetheart" Fern sighed, I won't call you Jack, but please boy, eat up! It'll make you grow big and strong!"

Little did Fern know that she'd inadvertently adopted an ogre toddler, and growing big and strong for him would have little to do with cabbages and more to do with live cows and stray children.

Every Day, Infinity

She was doomed to die too early, and was clearly on that track
but the reaper wasn't ready when my mother tapped his back
She'd said "Charon, you're a little late, I'm ready for my trip"
He'd said "Dear, you'll need to get in line,
there's no room in my ship"

She was years at death's apartment door, just knockin' every
day while her movements stilled a hundred fold, her pallor
turned to gray; and each day that she crept onward, we her
children grit our teeth for the dawns were filled with
questions; buy her flowers? or a wreath.

It was bless-ed sure, the days we had, each one a special gift
yet her weariness consumed us all, our lives were set adrift
I can only hope when my turn comes, it takes a single breath
for I'd save my dears the witness of a long and painful death.

Triquain Truth

Twin mirrors
one reflects contentment
the other seems imbued by darkness
a tiny twist in focus contorts perception
changes white to black, sweet to pungent
perfect sense, to nonsense
too often

Inevitability

She had desire for money, not enough, but twice that much
She worked at her religion, as a network, not a crutch
She took to social climbing, to enjoin a better class
And all that really stopped her was her husband,
"Horse's Ass"

My friends they tried to warn me,
they said "Boy, it's purely lust!"
"You're going to be a stepping stone,
she'll leave you in the dust!"
But I knew better, so I thought, and married her that day;
and I just ignored her wand'ring eyes that gazed so far away

I gave her what I had in stock, and what I had in store
I might have been a Rubick's Cube, but never was a bore
I went as far as corporate work, I even wore a tie
but even though I whored myself, my true love said goodbye

Public Face

Why is it in my heart I feel a weight I cannot daily bear
while in the glass my public face shows quite another mood
Is there no difference in the masks,
contented grin and vacant stare
How does my look speak confidence,
when conscience paints me crude

If I appear a pleasant sort, beware, I've donned a compromise
that I might mix with strangers and not send them off a mile
For oft' I bristle in my skin and ache to speak of tales unwise
ignoring rules of social grace, those soft reflected smiles

Ron Runeborg

Culture Creep

Herbert Delmange was not a happy Bloodletter. Since the first zombie had been allowed to buy acreage inside the boundaries of Full Moon Township, property values had plummeted; which of course led to more zombies being able to afford their own plot. For decades, Full Moon Meadows had been solely owned by Vampires and Lycanthropes. And then Bill Fleshrender had decided to pad his retirement nest egg by auctioning off his back 40 on Ebay.

"Who knew there was a wealthy zombie out there" Bill screamed as his neighbors burned down his house and blasted his family with silver bullets.

"Of course they're wealthy you moron, they've become computer programmers" Herbert chided his prisoner; "Why do you think they're always searching for brains! They're melted as fast as they can replace them!"

"I'm so sorry" Bill pleaded, "I didn't know!"

"Its too late for that now" Herb whispered as he pulled the trigger one last time. "We can't stop the zombification of Full Moon Meadows any more than we can keep the sun from rising. This neighborhood is going to Hell in a handbasket full of zombie parts, and Bill Fleshrender will go down in mythos as the fool who destroyed paradise."

Out Past Curfew

"Ok so we're on top of the world" Mortimer said. "What now smarty?"

Trudy slipped her left sleeve toward her shoulder and inspected her inner forearm scribbled crib notes again. "Find K2, and then look to the right."

Mortimer was beginning to whine. He wasn't exactly the best adventure partner Trudy might have considered.

"What is it we're looking for then, a great big neon arrow?"

"No mister crabby, we're looking for a rock formation that appears to be sleeping alligator"

"Hey! I was wondering what that was, look over there, I think I see it!"

The two young, novice angels flew toward the object, and true enough it did look just like an alligator's head and snout; though it could just as easily have been a pigs head prepared to roast. Trudy touched down near the stone-imal's large jaws and reached between its teeth. Hidden amidst the rocks was a small Celtic harp, which she extricated and began to play. Within moments a spotlight shone from the heavens, its beam encircling the little musician in a yellow/white glow.

"There's the back door, let's get cookin'" she said as she slipped the harp back into its chamber and flapped her wings until airborne.

"How long does it last?" Mort asked as he followed his mentor into the shaft of light.

"One minute earth time, so get your gown in gear, mister!"

Some People Just Can't Get Enough

My lungs were burning, my legs cramping; I was near the end of my endurance and scared out of my wits. I dodged, he stayed with me. Even my seemingly superhuman leaping over obstacles didn't faze him; it was like he was glued to my backside. I could feel his claws rasping at my shirt, smell the stench of rotted flesh and exposed organs.

Finally out of room, a 500 foot cliff before me, being eaten alive behind… I leapt, screaming, and fell, fell, fell, landed. Convulsing, I threw myself off the mattress and woke from the dream on the hard floor of my room.

I peered under the bed, spotting his beady little red eyes.

"What the hell is wrong with you" I said angrily, "don't I play with you enough in the daytime?"

"I was bored" said my boogyman. "Go back to sleep and this time I'll let *you* chase **me**!"

With the Crown's Permission

Mortimer cleaned and then sharpened his blade. It had been a long day of whacking here and whacking there; it seemed like the work would never end. How many traitors could there be in one kingdom, he wondered.

"Would ya rub a little liniment into me biceps lass" he called to his wife Betunia, "I'm crampin up a bit."

Betty pulled up a stool next to her man and wet her hands with smelly oil. As she massaged his massive muscles she noted he wasn't his normal self.

"Usually my dear you are overwrought after a day of executions, flooded with guilt for what you've been party to. You seem so relaxed! Why should today be any different?"

"The King has a royal 'and in my demeanor my love" he answered with a shrug. " 'e's begun calling these 'Casual Fridays', and thus 'as removed the angst from me weary shoulders!"

"I'm so happy for you my sweet; that's so kind of His Majesty" Betty sighed.

"Well" said Mort, "I still favor 'Titular Tuesdays' when I'm lopping the 'eads of nobilities. I'm 'appy to suffer guilt when such deserving necks are severed! But it's nice to 'ave a day to be indifferent altogether."

The 97% Solution

It made me laugh when I recognized the room. Nothing had changed in the 20 years since I'd been there last; even the same paint was peeled in the same corners. Of course, when my mother was in psychiatric lockup it was because of a breakdown having to do with a disease, something far easier to comprehend, even with the little green men and talking dogs. This time it was my father, the man with no fear, the great Scandinavian stoic who had suffered a lifetime of indignity with a raised head and focused eye.

They didn't even have a meeting room. There we were in the patient lounge, surrounded by cuckoo nesters, discussing what would become of daddy. It would be a come to Jesus meeting. We were to tell him everything we felt about his suicide attempt and explain to him that this was objectionable and then, presumably, his depression would vanish with a puff of smoke and the flight of a pair of suddenly appearing doves.

"He needs someone to talk to besides his children," I said; "he needs camaraderie with people who have lived through similar tragedy and survived."

The shrink on duty explained that while there may be some therapy involved, 97% of depression was dealt with through chemistry. It was then I decided that if that's what the world had come to, suicide wasn't necessarily unacceptable after all.

A Tragic Circumstance

"We need you Schmitty, the paramedics are unloading and we'll need to move right away."

Thomas Schmidt stood silently, staring down the frozen rail toward the instrument of death that he alone was certified to pilot. He knew he'd need to move, but at that moment felt paralyzed, able to do little more than in and ex-hale the ice crystals that permeated the pre dawn, sub zero air. The thrumming of the diesel engine hypnotized, its scent still noticeably pungent even after 26 years as a rail engineer. Perhaps it was the quickly freezing blood downstream that gave an extra harshness to the smell of the switchyard, maybe the engine was running rough once having killed one of its own.

"I saw the whole thing Levi; I saw his torso hit the ground. I should have been able to stop man, I tried, God knows I tried."

Levi Brown gently put his hand on the man's shoulder. The preacher they'd called him, as he'd talk the mission gospel while he worked. Not that he actually preached to anyone in particular, but that his exclamations were always peppered with "Thank you Jesus" and "Halleluiah".

"God knows Thomas; you can't stop a train with a flick of your wrist. Now let's go man, Ernie's out there, even though he's surely dead we can't leave him lying in the snow."

"What if he's...?" Though he couldn't finish the sentence, the thought was enough to make Thomas start the walk back, carefully sliding across the ponds of ice that had developed on both sides of the track, ice from snow turned to water by the heat of friction from passing train wheels. Ernie couldn't be alive, it was impossible. Calling an ambulance was simply an exercise in futility, Thomas had watched every second of the accident as if he'd known in advance where to keep his attentions.

The paramedics were waiting as he and Levi approached, and the four men climbed aboard Chicago & Northwestern 184, hauled up a stretcher and trauma kit and got underway. It seemed surreal having to travel a few hundred yards in a diesel engine but the yard was packed this January; only the main line and tracks seven and twelve were open at all, and the derailment had happened on twelve. It would have been hard enough for medics to reach the spot in the summertime, walking the rails at night was a daunting task for even those men that did it to feed their families. With snowpack and ice filling the gaps between one track and another, and the looming boxcars, 20 feet from ground to catwalk blocking out all residual light, there was no choice but to chauffer the docs to the site of the tragedy. It was doggedly slow, but at least possible.

Thomas was very cautious on the throttle, now gun shy and worried if he'd ever again be able to stop a train; worried that it might have been his age or inattention or lack of ability that had created this mess. Hell, it may have even been just his bad luck, but it was a part of him now, as much as he was a part of it. His foreman switchtender was dead, crushed in half, and it was his hand at the controls when it had happened.

They reached the site within a few minutes and Levi and the medics jumped from the wide step at the base of the engine, running through the snow to jump over a knuckle connecting two cars on track eight. There would be four knuckles to cross, four wide pieces of rusting iron, like giant, clenching fists three feet off the ground. They were too wide to straddle, yet the metal was so cold that touching it with bare skin would automatically incorporate your body part to the machine. So it took a little maneuvering to make each passage, all the more time consuming if there were indeed a snowball's chance in hell it mattered.

Thomas watched Levi's flashlight vanish as the shadow of the last medic grew to silo size and then winked out. It would be at least ten minutes, if there was anything that remained that might be collectable. It hadn't appeared so.

It didn't surprise him that his recall was in slow motion as that was how the original scene had played out. Ernie was hanging onto the last car's ladder, halfway to its roofline, waving his lantern to signal distance between he and the train they would attach onto. Three waves with the lantern, three box car lengths, and Thomas cut the throttle back a notch, slowing the entire train to a couple miles an hour. Pushing a train was always a noisy process, on the push the cars would clank together and as the speed dropped each car would slam apart. Quiet was the sign of a good crew, though only strived for silently as no one would openly admit trying to micro manage hundreds of tons of steel and a few thousand horsepower. Ernie's crew was generally as quiet as switchyard crews get. Not that there was a prize for being dainty; like all jobs on the railroad the faster you move the better the company likes you. It was more a relief from boredom that Schmitty would touch the throttle as if it were a woman's fishnet stockinged leg, and twist it as if he were removing a bullet from his own… slow and certain, calmly, with all senses heightened.

It's why he knew what was happening almost before it happened. He could almost hear the gravel roadbed give way, the tiny rocks pinging against each other in their rush to escape the weight of a hundred boxcars. He thought he heard the rending of a half dozen ties, the creosote soaked timbers exploding as if termite infested and dynamite rigged. He was sure he heard the rail clang, an unmistakable sound that travels through the air as if an arrow, the sound of tie pins snapping and a steel track being thrown outward by a tonnage too extreme to deny.

As the rear car derailed he swallowed his tongue or he'd for sure have shouted to Ernie to watch out. Like the last person on an ice rink whip, Ernie was tossed free of his handhold by the jostling of the heavy metal and landed on the frame of a hopper car on the next track, only a few feet away. He'd been spun midair and his body had disappeared in the open pocket between the hopper itself and the cars main girders, but the backs of his knees had hung up on a cross beam, and there he dangled a foot off the ground; for only a few seconds.

Thomas sucked in two lungsfull of frigid air as he remember the next moment, the coming together of two trains, the explosion of flesh, crushed between unforgiving, relentless steel plate. He screamed, just as he had when it happened; only this time he let it loose and screamed until he could barely catch his breath.

A lantern beam swung from the ground to the engineer's window; the three had returned and two were carting a stretcher between them.

"He's alive for Christ sake! Thomas, he's alive!" Levi shouted so loud that Schmitty winced at the power in his voice. "We're on board get our asses outa here before we lose him!"

It was only a few minutes back, but it seemed a lifetime in hell. Thomas could not let it go, that the man barely breathing on the catwalk just outside his window, the half a man barely breathing, was injured because of some inefficiency on the engineer's part. That his living would be no less an indictment, in fact perhaps more punishing as he would have incredible difficulty, pain, expense, and Thomas would carry at least a portion of the blame.

He was in a daze when he stepped off the engine. Levi and the paramedics had unloaded their charge and the ambulance was just pulling out of the "Q" yard's driveway as Thomas stepped to the ground.

The yardmaster and the rest of Ernie's crew was inside the yard office, all either crying or muttering obscenity, though Levi was praying while he cried. A handful of "It wasn't your fault Schmitty"s were spoken, yet they never registered as absolution. Thomas walked to the time clock, punched out, then slipped his card back into its slot before turning and leaving the building. It would be the last time he'd cross that threshold; the last time he'd drive from his farm into the city. Yet never came the last time he'd suffer his nightmare, nor came an ounce of self-forgiveness, for simply being in the wrong place at the wrong time.

Cataclysm

Sunday had passed into Monday as the full moon reached the top of its arc and started down the other side of the sky. I'd been napping behind my computer in my writing shack; too sick with fever to do anything constructive, but too stiff to walk to the house and slip into my bed again. Every 20 minutes or so I'd raised my head and clicked my email button, watching with blurred vision as my outlook express cycled through to the "you got nothing sucker" banner.

It was quiet in my studio, only the occasional thump of my forehead into the desk breaking the silence. And then, there was a scratch at the door.

It was deadly cold outside, at least in the 20s below zero. Anything that was alive and non-polar must have been hanging onto existence by a thread. Out of curiosity, I swung the interior door open and flicked on the outside light. Looking up at me through my glass storm door, licking the frost off its chin was a raccoon sized black cat. "C'mon man lemme in" he said.

Sure, I should have noticed he spoke to me, since even in Minnesota cats don't usually talk. But like I said, I was sick and a little woozy and it seemed like a reasonable request since it was terribly cold; so I opened the door.

The moment I'd given him room he burst inside and across the top of my pool table, ripping its cover to the floor while scrambling to get to the computer desk. Leaping from one counter to another the animal pounced onto my corded electronic laser mouse and with one swipe of his long, sharp claws, ripped through the tiny cord and dragged the device to the floor.

The sound was incredible, my eardrums popped twice in the barrage of ultra high frequency as the beast shrieked in glee and tore at the plastic with all four paws. He and his gray pray flopped about my floor like dying salmon in the bottom of a rowboat, and yet with all the power he could muster he never disassembled his target. I just watched at distance, not that I was pleased with having my property ransacked; I was more worried about what might happen to my face if I bent over and said "Bad Kitty, drop that right now!"

He seemed to lose his breath, he slowed and finally stopped, laying on his side and gently picking at the plastic as if he were suddenly overcome by depression.

"It's a computer mouse you moron; it's not to eat" I stated with an added grunt of disgust.

"I, I'm sorry" he mewed, "I saw you playing with it through the window and, well, I just wanted a little taste. It's so cold; I'm so hungry... forgive me?"

He was a cat, I was powerless.

"Well, if you keep..."

"Hey! Is that microwave popcorn?" He yowled as he again leaped to my pool table, tearing its uncovered fabric to shreds on his way to the box of Orville Redenbacher "Real Butter".

It was going to be a long night.

Ron Runeborg

A Guy Just Knows

She was mopey, yet angry. Oh it wasn't exaggerated; she's as subtle as a panther on a hunt.

"What's wrong honey" I asked, flinching a bit so as to steel myself for what would surely be a blowout. She just looked at me and remained silent. Yea, you know the look. Only this one said so many things, if it were a mood ring it'd have a pot of gold and its leprechaun inside it.

I guess I should have investigated further, but I figured her silence meant I was her focus; it was something I'd done. As we sat there at the kitchen table I racked my brain for answers; something I might apologize for before she'd need to fashion it into a 2 x 4 and use it to whack me upside the head.

It could have been something I'd said; hell, how many hours go by without my inadvertently saying something to tick her off. But I was reasonably certain that the past 48 hours had been gaffe free. In fact, I'd been particularly nice to her of late. Just yesterday I'd given her a little Hello Kitty lip gloss for giggles, and she did.

There was something between us that I'd always suspected was a point of friction; my being friends with women. Sure, we discussed it before we married. I just happen to like women better than men. Yes, their minds, not their breasts… necessarily. (I mean I sometimes like their breasts too but not in that way, and I always like their minds more) She says she's fine with that, she doesn't feel threatened at all, she knows I love her; but I've always harbored doubts, even though she has male friends and I'm just fine with that.

So maybe that was it. Maybe the fact that I spent last evening reminiscing about high school glory days with Cindy Statler made her jealous. Maybe she imagined the two of us, you know, intrawebbing body parts. Well, I don't know what to say about that, it's not like I've never thought about it before. But honestly, I've never laid a finger on her, nor would I; probably because I know she'd tell all her friends. No, no, that's not the reason. Oh that must be it. I supposed I should open a discussion about last night to see if that was the cause of her pout. But before I could say a word, she spoke in a teeny, shuddering voice.

"You know that bible study class I do on Saturdays? You know, with Molly and Silva and Rachel and Steph?"

"I do," I replied. "Ruth's circle isn't it?"

"Yea, well, we don't really study the bible."

My heart sank. Maybe she cheated on me once a week. Maybe it was that guy, what's his name, Gerry?

"If you have something to tell me, please just spit it out" I said forcefully.

"The five of us rob banks" she said.

Well, *there* was something I hadn't considered.

Ron Runeborg

Desert Sailor

He might have been all of 14. Normally, I wouldn't have noticed, but there was something wrong with his gait. He wasn't limping so much as laboring; as if he was struggling under a great weight. I yelled at him to stop, but of course, I don't know Arabic. I thought the right word was tawaqqafa, but for all I know I was yelling "You may eat the kumquat."

It was the coat that gave me goose bumps. Sure it was autumn, but it really wasn't that cold and most of the villagers I'd seen went about their business in woolen shirts or light vests. This was a pea coat, something I'd never seen before in Halmut province, or anywhere in country for that matter. Add to that a really odd sight; the coat bulged out as if the kid was fat. There are no fat people here. He would have been the first I'd witnessed in my 8 month tour.

I'm sure I decided within a few seconds, but it seemed like a lifetime. Shoot a teenager? A kid? Has it come to this? I sprayed a few rounds in the air and shouted for him to stop once more, but he didn't seem to hear me. He could have been deaf, maybe so accustomed to guns going off that he was unfazed. No matter. He was close by then, 30 feet I guessed and still advancing. So I aimed for his body and let loose. As I pulled the trigger all I could think was "he's just carrying a sack of rice, or a goat, or he actually is the only fat kid within a hundred miles of this checkpoint."

The explosion threw me over our Humvee. At least I was the only one hurt, besides the kid who pretty much disintegrated. But he'd made his choice… and had forced me to make mine.

Riverboat King

Every 17 year old boy needs a place to go when, you know, when the world gets to be too big. I had to guess most of them had "their rooms". I hadn't had a room for some time. Oh, I had a basement and a bed now and then, but between me and the spiders it wasn't a place I'd go for comfort. The floors I'd slept on weren't private enough, the closets too cramped and my car, well my car was for transportation and napping, not for contemplating life.

I'm sure many would use study hall or the back of the stage in the school auditorium where the audio visual club stored their ancient equipment; or the gym, under the bleachers. But see, I'd already dropped out, and while I could have snuck inside, were I caught I would be treated as a common criminal rather than a needy citizen. So, that was off limits too.

I used the woods as often as not. There are thousands of little woodlands in the Twin Cities, most of which one could disappear into for at least a day or two. But you had to keep your eye out for other trespassers; criminals laying low, hobos hoping to catch a stray dog and make a stew, winos sleeping off their last drunk, and feral men, prowling with their noses, seeking the scent of random lost boy.

No, the best place for me, particularly when I could witness the dawn on the back end of the day was West River Road between Franklin Avenue and the West Bank of the University of Minnesota. The road itself was like a giant scoop, dropping vertically perhaps 100 feet to the river bottoms, and then rising again before scooting into the hospital complex where my mother had found living space as a resident crazy.

The riverbank sloped gradually but steeply if you get my drift, the street was wide, the boulevard, nearly as wide again and the shoreline boasted a half wall of stone and concrete, probably built in the 30's by the WPA. It was there I'd plant my butt, feet dangling over the rushing, muddy water, face to the east, in wait for the almighty yellow star.

When you need a meditation spot, it's all about aesthetics. At 4 AM all you could hear was the low hum of power pole transformers and the trickling of thousands of cubic feet of liquid passing by on its way to Mexico. Across the way, the Josia Snelling riverboat waggled in the current, sending out little splashes of foam. To the south the Franklin bridge stood in the twilight and occasional clickity clacks served notice that a rare car was crossing its expansion jointed surface.

And to the north, well, that's where I first spotted what I knew to be a body. Ok, "know" is a strong word. Let's say I guessed it was and my intuition proved to be dead on so to speak. Of course it was a body, I figured; it'd be just my luck to have my meditational moment ruined, not that whoever had been the live person that belonged to this floating lump hadn't had worse luck than I, considering the dead part.

It was at least 600 yards away, just turning the corner after St. Anthony Falls, but still I recognized the size and shape from the excess bobbing and the splay of its extremities. It, he, she, whatever, was face down, fully clothed in some sort of slacks and plaid coat, arms and legs spread as if falling from an airplane and trying desperately to slow its descent.

And it was twirling for the first hundred feet or so, like a spin art card at the State Fair.

Yes, I knew I should run to the nearest pay phone and call someone. But, I didn't. I just sat there and watched another lost soul make its lazy way downstream. It wasn't that I was stunned. Though having dead bodies float past wasn't a daily occurrence, I had seen death and its bitter results by then; often enough that my little heart wasn't so much as set a-flutter. And the police and I had been at crossed purposes for a year or two, so I was in no rush to become a "good citizen" for the sake of law and order. Besides, there was another issue. What if this guy didn't want to be found?

This wasn't the way I'd have picked to go out. Over the time I'd contemplated cliff jumping. I'd developed a plan that would have made my death an anonymous thing, a simple disappearance, easily forgotten and set aside. Still, it seemed a lot of suicides were public events, a leap from a tower, a belly flop off a bridge, a speeding car into a brick wall. Yet you always wonder if the person committing the act somehow thought their body would be swallowed up by the earth, so their loved ones wouldn't need to identify it and then adding insult to injury, pay for the disposal of it. It could be the case here I thought. The Ford dam was just a few miles downstream. Chances were great that left alone the body would become trapped in the works and never be seen again.

As what was obviously a man's body passed in front of me, swerving a bit eastward into the barge channel as it slid by, I did recognize the possibility that this was no suicide at all. It could be a drunk who fell off a bridge, or a homeless guy who tumbled down the riverbank after reaching for the remains of a discarded fast food hamburger that happened to be just a little too far out of reach.

Oh sure, he could be a murder victim too; a mafia guy shot for snitching or a loan shark customer late on his payments, and since I couldn't tell the skin color, it could have been a white or black guy wandering into the wrong neighborhood as the river separated the two a ways upstream.

By the time I noticed the sun had risen, it was already forcing me to squint. I'd missed the moment; the ritual gathering of strength to face the future had been frittered away, like the life that once belonged to dead guy in the river.

I had to wonder then; if the naysayers were right, there was nothing after death and what was rapidly moving out of my sight range was just chemicals in a skin leisure suit. Were some Eastern religions correct, I had no doubt this guy would come back as a fish. Were my people correct, he'd either be in Heaven or Hell already, or at that time, Purgatory, the waiting room for the spiritually ambivalent or mediocre.

And then, just as I wished him swift passage into whatever comes next, he was gone, and I was again completely alone. He did kind of ruin my morning, but at least he'd kept me company. I was lonely enough by that point in my life, even dead people could befriend me without my turning them away.

There was little point in sitting there any longer. The world's scars show up in the light of day; the riverboat's chipping paint, the graffiti on the half wall, the garbage in the street. The magic had ended, the next show wouldn't be for another

23 hours. As I stood and walked toward my motorcycle, I promised dead guy I'd call the cops, though I did explain that I wouldn't be leaving my name and number, and that I'd have to wrap my lips around a bottle of something first, so I could be on the phone with the enemy and stay relaxed and focused. It was the first and last time I'd regretted not bringing alcohol to my special place. It was the first and last time I'd felt the need to be removed of the weight of the planet by chemical alteration while standing on that hallowed ground. It was a little ironic really. Water, water, everywhere; and not a drop to drink.

If you can't say anything nice

Podrick Bunt was quite thorough in his evaluation. After all, the king himself had invited him as the foremost art critic in all of Westrose to give council on a gallery of paintings.

"This is awful!" he exclaimed, "and this! This is an abomination! Sire! I beg you to burn these ungodly dung heaps as it is obvious the artist is a complete twit!" And so his critique rattled on, until at last none of the 35 paintings displayed were unsullied by the master's harsh words.

The next morn as Illan Flatwater approached the castle he took note of the head of his rival Podrick Bunt hanging from the castle barbican. The foremost art critic in all of Eastrose was nervous indeed, having been called to council the king on matters of the canvas. Yet he had a leg up on Sir Podrick, or a skull up as it were. He'd already been told of the king's newest passion, painting by numbers.

Ron Runeborg

Bona Fide Bloodhound

Others didn't seem to have my problem. As far as I could tell each had theirs snuggly packed away in their garages, or their kitchen cabinets, or wherever people kept such things. Mine? Mine was let loose on this mountain trail, and it was up to me to catch it on my own.

It's not like I wasn't offered a share of at least a dozen others' versions. In fact, people had been cajoling me for weeks to just consider theirs' my own. But I was having none of it. No matter how cozy I got with someone else's it would never belong to me. So I ran; up, left, over rocks, through trees. I ran so hard I almost passed out, and then I crawled. I had the scent, I knew it couldn't elude me entirely, but I had to overtake it and frankly, I thought I might die trying. Still, I had to follow my father's advice to honor his memory. He'd always said, "never give up when in pursuit of the truth."

I can hear it just over the next ridge, laughing at me as I wheeze my way up this hill. I wonder if it's worth it, if the truth is all that special. All I know is when I get hold of it I'm not going to let it see daylight for a month. I'm far more comfortable saying "I knew it all along" than "No, you're wrong, I have the truth right here…"

Simply Pants

It's not easy being a pair of pants; the term itself proves that my very existence is misunderstood. Why, I'm a single organism, an individual being! There's no two of me in the universe, (though I will admit to having seen cheap imitations of my svelteness on the streets). So let's get over it people! I'm not a pair! I am simply PANTS!

Again I say, it's not easy being pants. For one, I always have to worry if my zipper's down. I'm fond of shouting "Hey up there, I can't pull the damn thing up by myself you know! I'm just PANTS!!!" But of course, humans can't understand clothics, nor can they hear the frequencies at which we speak.

Shirt laughs at me when I yell; he thinks I just like the sound of my own voice. "Well maybe that's so" I've told him; "I do enjoy the vibrations created by my bottom register". He only answers "Well if your patron didn't have such a large bottom, perhaps you'd not have such a deep tone!"

I like shirt. He has a sense of place, you know. He's always trying to keep himself tucked in to my waistband. He says it's just that he feels more at home there, near undapants, but I think he's careful to not slop over my belt loops and cover up my marvelous pleats. After all, he came complete with French cuffs and collar tabs; it's obvious he has a wonderfully refined taste, by design. And my pleats are to die for, or so my human's girlfriend said when he modeled me at Sears big and tall shop.

Actually, I like nearly all my compatriots. Shirt's great, belt is snuggly and smells just like boots... in fact sometimes I can't help but think they're related, but they look so different; one brown, one light purple. I'd ask them but they're always too busy to talk; and I would hardly be inclined to interrupt belt when his sole purpose in life is to keep my buttons from popping by holding back the massive belly above him.

There is one pair of fellows though, that I'm not fond of; a cheeky sort of fabric, a gaggle of multicolored megalomaniacs if you were to ask me. It's socks I'm speaking of. Yes, both of them! Do you know what they did to me? Why just last winter when patron left the house to walk in a fresh snowfall, they insisted that they be pulled up and over my cuffs! Can you imagine? Rainbow striped, ten toed geeks! That's what they are! Somehow, patron heard them and stopped at a park bench to sit and pull socks up and over me. ME! So the snow wouldn't get in they said! Like I'd let snow get between me and legs!

I was so angry I lobbied for the threaded collective to convince patron that he didn't need socks; that it was far more fashionable to simply wear shoes *without* socks! And guess what! It worked! The human hasn't worn socks for months!

But as I said, it's not easy being pants; because now I have another problem. Shoes are really starting to stink. I suppose from having no socks to collect the sweat. Now I'd hardly mind, it's a small price to pay so as to show socks who's boss... but you can't imagine what it's like to be me when shoes stink. It's not like I can go anywhere. I'm like the last thing taken off every night, and the first thing on in the morning; unless he had sex and then undapants has the honor... well unless he had sex with himself and then undapants stays right where he is.

Undapants says he can't smell shoes. Me? I can't smell anything else for Old Navy's sake!

Darned socks! I hate socks! Life was good until SOCKS ruined everything!

Wainscot

I miss the days of city life, the smell of bread upon the breeze
The houses kept from crumbling by two extra coats of paint
The grand piano windows bearing glass of many colors high
on walls composed of lath and plaster, illustrating quaint

I miss the sound of sirens and the buzz of electricity
that hum along the power grid that whispers "I'm alive"
The people waiting for their bus,
the pets tied up at grocery doors
the vestige of "community" that suburbs just contrive

I miss the wainscot and the hutch,
the picture rail and papered walls
I miss the lousy floor plans with no closets and steep stairs
I miss the oak six panel doors,
 the windows masked in winter's frost
I miss the subtle dignity of life without its "airs."

I once created character from virgin cloth and memory
I tried to move a mountain with a shovel and a pen
At that I lost, and now I'm here in Placidville awaiting dark
yet reveling in those good thoughts of time lost passed again

Ron Runeborg

Simple Pleasures

My father had been in a virtual coma for three days, the combination of morphine and pain forcing his lifeless body to convulse on occasion, a muted groan leaving his lips every so often. The last I'd seen him functional was in the presence of my siblings and a lawyer, his signature needed to square up one item before his demise so as to keep the probate hounds at bay. A man with nearly perfect, feminine script was reduced to illegible scribble as he whipped off his "x" and fell fast asleep.

And now I sat next to him for the third day, my attentions drifting between Hollywood Squares and his shallow breathing, constantly wondering if I'd actually made my peace with the man who'd given his life to the cause of his wife and children.

"Wow" he said, eyes opened for the first time in days and smirky grin stretching his chapped lips. I turned and rest my hand on his shoulder as if to keep him from sitting upright, a pointless maneuver as he was far too weak to move voluntarily.

"What?" I answered softly, powering off the television. "What happened?"

"I was just thinking of the time you and I and Christopher (nephew/grandson) were in Japan, in the Kyoto gardens....how pretty it was...how peaceful. It was so real, as if we were still there, wandering the pebbled pathways. I laughed when the gardener chased off a pair of cranes who'd been dunking for fish in the koi ponds."

He chuckled a moment, then coughed, wincing back some sharp, derogatory report from an unidentified organ.

I smiled a curious smile and read the wonder in his eyes, the soft blue pools of insight that had watched me grow from hatchling to giant oaf. My palm slid from his shoulder to take his withered hand, his fingers barely able to grip mine in recognition.

"So that's where you've been" I said, doing everything in my power to not weep and ruin his one lucid moment.

He cocked his head a bit and raised an eyebrow, a favored affectation when he thought himself too clever. "We've never been to Japan have we?" he whispered, his words punctuated by a groan from deep within his cancerous body.

"Not yet" I said. I thought for a too long moment and added, "but it's on the list."

He smiled and lightly squeezed my hand. "You're a good kid" he said as he closed his eyes and returned to the red pine and boxwood flanked path, stopping at an ornate, red bridge to stand and watch plump, golden fishies; a final moment of pleasure before wandering off to meet his maker.

Ron Runeborg

The Grass in All Its Glory

These days are rife with clearing sales; those rows of trash upon the lawn and signs requesting quarters for a box of mismatched parts; the streets, alive with traffic, toting people to their weekday chores, to masters touting grindstone wheels for every willing nose.

These nights are filled with heavy sighs, and memories of youth now gone, of wasted opportunities, and scores of broken hearts; the streets, subdued, bereft of music save the twilight underscores and asymmetric keyboard clacks that turn the wind to prose.

Within the trash of humankind a rummage might find Avalon; a magic tome or marker that portends an altered start. A book perhaps, a tattered image bearing one to distant shores; a twist upon the life that is, toward that one might suppose.

And still each parcel of this ilk demands the price of brain or brawn; a penny for one's thoughts requires a penny must depart. So oft' we labor, tooth and nail, amidst the vapid teeming bores who dream of pretty pennies 'till their beings decompose.

Yet here while sorting silver clouds from sad conclusions long foregone, I fear atop my pennies wise lay horses, 'fore their carts. My joy is not commodity, no cash commands where spirit soars. My eyes once opened will absorb the depth of one red rose.

If I can but remember this, and hex commercial carrion my smile might spread more broadly twixt the goddess and her arts. If then to trash my lock box and step through those facing hundred doors I might again find rapture in those things a poet knows.

So help me now, you wunderkind, to see what's hidden by the dawn; the world that blazes far beyond these market cheats and charts. Take hold my hand and lead us to our soft and vibrant inner cores that we may know true meaning in the grass, and how it grows.

Fresh Meat

If I could be any non-mayonnaise sandwich,
I'd choose to be gouda and smoked Vermont ham
If I could be more of an elegant entrée,
perhaps I'd be succulent roast rack of lamb

If I could have any old moon watching partner
to wilt alongside as we gracefully aged
it just wouldn't do to have any but you
after all, you've the keys to my long rusted cage.

Ron Runeborg

Danse Cloudimalia

1: fire up your computer, then, step outside.
2: If it's a partly cloudy day, find 5 cloudimals and identify their species'.
3: Close your eyes, and imagine those animals in a circus with yourself as the Leprechaun animal trainer.
4: If one is a crocodile, make sure you're not lunch. If one of them is a dragon, make sure it breathes in the opposite direction.
5: Holding that thought, step back indoors and make your way to your writing office, the Whine Cellar.
6: Place your fingers on the keyboard and type ten times "They're magically delicious".
7: Now, make your animals do tricks within the periphery of your mind's eye while you write the first things that come to your mind.

My wife looked concerned. "Honey, I found this list on your desk. 'Making dragons breathe downwind?' What is this thing?"

"Oh it's just my writing checklist."

"Really. Does it have a title?"

"I call it "The Method to Useful Madness."

Choosing the Beautiful Lie

Meyrick Lewis stood at the oak plank bar of the Griffyn's Nest, surrounded by a dozen of his closest friends. He'd once thought that perhaps his buying the occasional round was all that framed his popularity, but only once; as popularity is a relative thing and only worth having, not worth discussing.

"Tell us about the missus again" Jenkin Burke said, and the boys all smiled and nodded their slightly tipsy heads.

"She's as fair as a bowl of fresh drawn shimmering cream" he began, choosing a different metaphor each time he was asked (and he had been asked each Friday night for as long as he could remember) "Her hair is a lustrous mahogany, smooth as a babe's and smelling of orchids and ginger."

"Ahh" moaned William McGee, "If only my wife had silky hair I'd want to tangle my fingers in it," he paused for dramatic effect, "rather than keep them in my pockets guarding my paycheck!"

"Aye!" The boys agreed, some laughing but others grimacing and shaking their heads at their bad luck.

"She's a regular chef you know" Meyrick continued; "why tonight when I get home she'll likely have made me a rack of lamb with potato and leek pie with a lovely Snowdon pudding for dessert."

Those assembled made smacking noises, as if tasting the delicacies through thin air. "You're a lucky man" Rees Blom said as he patted Meyrick on his back so hard the man had to stop to catch his breath.

"And what will she be wearin" Robert Hopkin asked.

"The usual" Meyrick said, as he had a hundred other times he'd been asked this delicate question; "You know, a gauzy material cut down to here and up to there. A gown that would appear as if nothing more than angel hair."

The resultant oohs and ahhs were interrupted by the clanging of the console clock that stood over Griffyn's Nest's fireplace hearth. It was ten, and well past time for a miner to be home and preparing for a night's rest. Meyrick took his leave cheerily, accompanied by well wishes and confessions of envy. The bicycle home was a whistling affair, a favored reel of his Irish grandfather.

His house was dark as he'd hoped. He climbed upon his stoop as quietly as he might, but still the moment he touched the door handle a light went on in the parlor. She would be awake then, there was no denying. He steeled himself and thrust the door open, stepping inside with a whoosh and slamming the door behind him. The clomp of the six panel was followed by a loud crash, and a spray of malted liquid spattered across his chest and face.

"At least she's missed" he thought to himself, though never saying a word. "My bones are still intact and I feel no blood oozing."

"Get your arse in here" the crone shouted, waving a second bottle in his direction, "and make me supper!"

"You've been out late again and left me here to starve you no good, rotten, less than a man!" She'd been at it again Meyrick noted; found the sauce he'd carefully hidden and worked herself into a lather.

"Yes, my love" he answered as he slipped off his waistcoat and walked toward the kitchen. He hadn't made it halfway before she was on him, punching and slapping until he could hold her tightly around the arms.

"As for your note" she spit through those teeth she still had within her wrinkled mouth, "I will bathe when I please and not before! If you don't appreciate my aroma then I suggest you wear a nose plug in me presence, you self-righteous bastard!"

"I'm so sorry my sweet, I don't know what got into me. Perhaps the coal dust in my lungs made me dizzy and near out of my mind. It won't happen again I assure you. Let me make you a nice bangers and mash."

She fell limp in his arms at that, and he let her free very slowly, setting her into an easy chair, keeping his head turned as he did in case she went for his eyes next.

"Be quick about it then" she croaked. "I'll not be treated like a common strumpet by my own husband!"

"Surely" Meyrick answered as he backed away and into the next room. There he closed the panel door and set about the business of boiling water and frying onion, all the while thinking of his next Friday adventure and the beautiful lies he'd tell, and all the smiles that would surround him.

Ron Runeborg

Baby, I'm a Vex Machine

"What does it **do**!" Jimmy was on me from the moment I unveiled my science project.

"It's a robot" I said, "can't you see any better than you can wipe your nose?"

"But, what's it dooo". He was using that whiny voice. The one he made louder and louder until everyone was looking at him. The one he used when he wanted to make fun of someone, make fun of me, no, humiliate me.

It was just a robot. It whirred and turned around and its jaw opened up and it made sounds like "arr" and "ghh" and stuff. It wasn't like Jimmy's mockup of the entire freaking universe with paper mache planets and marshmallow moons. My dad didn't have time or the money to make my science project better than anyone else's like Jimmy's did. Mine was just a robot.

"What's it doooooo!" Jimmy was on the chair now, pointing at me and laughing. I grabbed the robot and jumped as high as I could, whacking him on the head with it and knocking him clear off the chair and onto the floor where he lay unconscious.

"It's a flying pest exterminator" I said as I wandered off to await my punishment.

To His Honor

I was 13 and already I'd learned about the concept of honor. Sure, I'd also learned failure and disappointment, but I'd had a large helping of fortitude and commitment as well; commitment in all its meanings in fact.

As soon as my mother had driven off on her way to her mother's for the afternoon, my father had called a meeting. He'd never called a meeting before, it sounded silly, and yet we were all dreading the probabilities. My sisters were 12 and 10, and the three of us gathered in the dining room while my toddler brother locked his brain into memorizing commercial jingles on the television in the next room.

"Obviously your mother and I have been having problems," he began.

Yea. Problems. Like the sheriff showing up on Christmas eve to take mom to the nuthouse. That was a problem. Like the constant screaming, the smashing furniture, the wielded weapons and the continual accusations; he cheated with the church women, with the neighbors, with the neighbor's daughter, with her sisters, he was a sex machine, a penisaur, a regular Johnny Appleseed. Yea, those were problems. None of us had spoken about the particulars. I knew he was innocent as well as I knew anything, but even then I was addicted to the idea that there are no absolutes so I was forced to wear a nagging doubt around my neck like a dead and rotting albatross that stunk to high heaven. My siblings on the other hand, I had no idea what they thought. I only knew they disagreed with me on nearly all matters of importance (and even those of no importance at all) so it was likely they assumed their father was a scumbag.

"I'm sad and worried about what this is doing to you guys, and I don't see many options as to how to fix what's broken."

My stomach started to rotate, top to bottom, like it didn't want to hear what was coming next so it was covering its tummy ears by squishing them into my intestines.

"I think I should move out."

My stomach suddenly flopped back into position, but I thought it had gotten caught on my guts along the way as I nearly puked right there. The girls were teary eyed. Nancy cried a lot, so that didn't surprise me, though when she'd cry I found it damned hard not to cry myself so I prayed that she would just sniffle a little and let it go at that. Barb on the other hand, even if she cried I couldn't care, because if she did I was pretty sure it would be tears of joy that Nancy and me were in pain and suffering as that was the entire root of her miserable life.

He went on for another 20 minutes I think, though I was kind of floating off the ground so it's hard to tell if my time sensors were working right. He explained that he'd already looked at an apartment up in the Lowry Hill area and it was crappy and hot, but close to work so he could leave the car with mom and walk because it would be really tough financially but he thought he could make do and all that.

I visualized him in an apartment. Some shabby couch would be in the living room with a lamp next to it; on the floor since there wouldn't be any end tables. Just a couch, and a tv, if he could even afford a tv. Maybe that would have to wait. And then the bed would be out of my grandparents' attic, that teeny thing I had to sleep on when I'd go do yard chores all day and have to sleep over even though the bed was made for a Japanese guy and I'm tall like Frankenstein. And there he'd be I figured, most of his day when he couldn't beg an extra shift off the post office, just staring at the wall and wondering what life was for since it obviously wasn't for what he'd thought it was.

"But I wanted to let you guys have a vote in it. You're young, but this will affect you as much as me. You'd have to live with mom and go to school just like you do now. I couldn't take any of you with me, and I wouldn't want to do that to your mom anyway; she loves you very much you know, even though she doesn't show it lately."

I knew that. I always knew it. Even when she was stark raving mad she loved her little Ronnie. And I knew it would kill her to not have us there. And of all the things I wanted my mom to be at that point, dead wasn't one of them.

"So I want you guys to vote. I need you to tell me what you think. Should I go? Would you be ok if I went? We'd see each other all the time, you don't have to worry, I'll visit and I'll have you over and we'll go on Sunday drives like always… but, what do you think?"

There wasn't even a breath taken between his question and our response. It was clear, and immediate. "Yes" we all said at once.

Why my sisters said it, I couldn't be sure. I only knew how I felt. My dad leaving would tear my heart right out of my chest; but watching him slowly die, his soul eaten away by the acid of my mother's mental illness, was killing me outright. I couldn't stand to see him suffering anymore, trying to let it roll off his back only to have it fill his boots and weigh him down to the point of paralyzation. I wanted him to go even though I would then be the man of the house, responsible for all that man stuff that my mother wouldn't be able to do. Maybe I'd become the target of her rage. Oh please God, let her skewer me and give dad a break. If only.

"Yes" we said again. And we all cried, except for David, who was busy repeating the last six McDonalds commercials he'd seen word for word.

He never did go. He couldn't. We, including mom, were his responsibility, and he just had to work it out. And none of us complained. I was only glad to have been there, to let him get his burden off his chest for one hour of one day. To his honor.

Nibblin on Bacon, Chewin on Cheese

Thaddeus sank into the mud and sighed heavily. It was the worst of luck, a most humiliating turn of events. His newborn son… " 'e's a mutant 'e is!" The words of midwife Moll made him angry enough to chew his way through an entire forest, yet as his rank required, he just glared at her and let it pass.

He turned to his wife Emma and whispered "Our son's not a mutant… is he?"

"Oh no silly" Em answered, "not at all. He's just… sensitive! The doctor said in every other way he's a perfect little beaver. He's just…"

"Allergic to tree bark, yes I heard don't say it again PLEASE!"

Emma nuzzled her man. "Don't worry so, precious. I called my cousin Samantha and she's agreed to teach him her family ways if we approve. He'll be much happier there I think."

That was the last straw. Thad reared onto his tail, standing him six inches above his already imposing thirty two inch height. "No son of mine is gonna be a RODENT! He's a BEAVER damn you all!"

But he knew, as he wandered off for the night, that it was the boy's only option; and at sunset he gave Emma permission to start teaching him his cousin's ways by singing him the anthem he would need to swear to follow… "Muskrat Love."

A Pragmatic Betrothal

"I'm pregnant" she said, anticipating.

"I'm sterile" I said, "did I forget to tell you?"

"Damn you" she screamed, anticipation turning to rage.

"Do you want me that badly?"

"No, but you're a better meal ticket."

"I've always admired your honesty," I said; "I'll think about it."

CONsequence

All his life Jerry had done the right thing, the honorable thing. He was a good man, compassionate, even benevolent his neighbors would say.

"It wasn't a con Jerry, just small type," said Cliff the mortgage banker.

"You'll not have my home" Jerry said as he pulled the trigger.

The Mothers As Well

Mio stood on the Ada Ciganlija dock, watching the Sava River as it flowed past the island and through the city to meet with the Danube. The official's boat had left the Fortress already and the president would be passing the Belgrade fairgrounds and into Mio's view within minutes. He raced to make his final decision; he weighed every choice, advocated every devil and still came to the same conclusion. There had been enough bloodshed; the war was beyond the borders of purpose and into the realm of genocide. The president must be removed.

Surely others were thinking the same, others within the homeland, even the party. But no one had the access of the president's personal bodyguards; no one would ever get closer to the butcher but the butcher's wife. And the butcher's wife idolized her shouting shopkeeper; there would be no relief delivered from her hand.

He'd thought to wait. In fact he'd thought to wait for a year now, hoping that someone could squeeze a single bullet through the walls of flesh that Radovan surrounded himself with daily. But it was fruitless; those that didn't agree with city hall were crushed under its bricks and mortar, those that had attempted to use politics or even currency to sway an assassin to the task were rooted out by shadow police and stripped of their skin.

He'd loved his work; he had always been ruthless and cold, considering death to be a remarkably fair arbiter between those that have and those that desire. But he'd always felt comfortable within the boundaries of hell, where evil men plotted against evil men to pilfer ill-gotten gains. His duties had begun in that style four years past, but things were different now; the war had changed everything including Mio's view of the bigger picture. He'd never noticed there was such a thing, until he'd watched a grieving mother lifted from her eight year old son's grave by a 50 caliber bullet, and flung two yards across the freshly turned soil; until he'd delivered a message from his employer to a general in the field, and there watched as 30 children's bodies were pushed into a ditch by a tractor bearing a snow plow, all to be drowned in diesel fuel and set on fire.

Mio checked his gun one last time as the cruiser maneuvered into its slip and the dignitaries on board prepared to disembark. The right moment would come, he would know it, and he would be quick about it. Perhaps his act would have no consequence; no one could be sure what kind of leader would follow this one, it could well be an even more brutal megalomaniac. But the odds were even that there would be an uprising of those Serbs of good conscience were this monster to be silenced, and even odds were better than guaranteed loss.

The ride to the island's shooting range was pleasant enough, Mio took his position in the front passenger seat and the president and his 5 cronies filled the rear, busily telling jokes and drinking bourbon throughout the fifteen minute drive.

The parking area in front of the range office was filled with soldiers, just as the docks had been. Security was very tight always, but during the conflict it had become nearly impenetrable; there were more soldiers assigned to the country's politicians than serving in any single unit in the field.

It is difficult to prosecute a war when so many of your own population would like to see you dead.

Were it any other man, the show of force would have stopped him. But Mio had already accepted his fate. He would die, there was no doubt; and perhaps in his act he would have atoned for his past. But either way he would be a martyr to a more civilized Serbia, a free and strong Serbia wherein the stains of centuries of bloodletting could be washed from its foundations at last.

The governmental party prepared to take their positions for the competition, clay pigeons had been stacked, springs oiled, shells loaded and boxed. For nearly an hour the six men blew earthen plates into chalk, toasted each other's fine abilities and boasted of tournaments won. And then Mio found his moment.

"Another bottle Mio" Karadzic had called to him. "Bring me another quickly!"

The case of American whiskey lay open against a wall beyond the president. To reach the box, Mio would pass directly behind his target and within three feet or less of the back of his head. This was his time; he took a deep breath and held it as he strode confidently toward his boss while waving his acknowledgement. Three steps hence he pulled his automatic from its holster and swung to his right as all hell broke loose.

Csilla knelt over her son's casket and touched the splintered wood at the place behind which his face might be hiding. She blew him a kiss through the river of her tears, and her

husband Gabor squeezed her shoulder more firmly as he too
spent his grief.

"Your son was a traitor" Karadzic spat as he lifted his Ruger
to the head of the weeping man. "I knew it all along; I could
see his weakness in his eyes. He'd lost his will to hate."

True Secrets of the Birds and Bees

I often wish I were not really real,
but a fiction, a creature, a dream
A unicorn maybe, a kite in the sky
or a big bowl of melting ice cream

I'd gladly be bad if that's all I could choose
like, say Skeletor, Riddler or Gollum
I'd rather be kind but I'd take anything
that would make me more fun and less solemn

If I let you be, say an elkhound on skis
would you downhill to where I could morph?
Would you play if I let you be Queen of the Elves?
Would you make me your bodyguard Dwarf?

Sure, I often wish there were no rules at all
and our likeness would change with the breeze
then you could present the sum knowledge of birds
and in turn I'd espouse for the bees

The Ring of Morosity

I had just been jettisoned from the "Third Planet" species production mold when God sat me atop a carousel horse and gave its behind a little tap. As you would suspect, a little tap from God is hardly little, but the horsy took it in stride and joined his brethren in the slipstream with only a halfhearted yelp. Around and around we went for some reason unbeknownst to me at that moment.

Then as if sensing my complete confusion horsy whispered, "grab a ring for heaven's sake." Ring? I looked about. Sure enough, just at the apex of my most distant reach was a series of brass rings, each marked in day glow colors with coded nametags stating various emotions.

"Do these signify something?"

"They are your personality traits" said Horse; "your first experience with free will, though in this case there's a little fun involved. Usually it's not so fun."

"And what, I grab one? And then?"

"You get three actually. And whichever you snatch, stay with you forever! So aim carefully!"

Well, there was no way I was losin out on this deal, so I climbed up onto Horsy's back to be closer to my targets. A fetus' arms are very short as you know, so every inch I could add would be a godsend... so to speak.

There it was! I'd spotted "Amusement" and had to have it! I almost jumped from my perch but held tight to the pole with my left hand as I grabbed with my right. Shit! Missed! And accidently hooked the next in line!

"Whadja get?"

Crap! "I got "Stress".

"Nice shot bucko. Better try for sleepiness next. Maybe they'll counter each other."

"Har de har!" I was miffed, but not beaten. I looked for another that might move me up the champion ladder. One perfect trait nearly went by so I snagged it quickly.

"Courage" I shouted! "I got courage!"

"Funny" said Horse. "There's only one of each and there goes courage to that fat kid; perhaps you misread it"

I looked at the inscription on my second ring. Heck in a handbasket!

"Powerlessness" I mumbled. "Great, I've already screwed up my life and I haven't even seen the sky yet."

"Don't worry pal" said Horsy, "there's one left that will make the others moot if you can get it."

What's that" I asked.

Horse pointed with his right hoof. "Happiness. A happy person can make positives out of negatives! You might be stressed and powerless, but if you're happy, you won't give a crap cuz, well cuz, you'll be happy!"

Horse had a point. I had to get the happy ring. We spun around and around while I focused in on my prize. I flexed my chubby little fingers a hundred times, reached out with my chubby little arms until I felt as if I'd stretched another 6 inches into them. And then, I took aim, thought positivity thoughts (though I was a little stressed) and took a last grasp at "happiness."

I closed my eyes and showed the ring to Horse. "Tell me what it says, I can't look."

Horse made that lip flappy sound. Then he said "What does morosity mean?"

Well, it wasn't happiness, but maybe it was something that would make me special at least. I jumped off Horse and ran for the library with my new personality. I had a date with a dictionary.

Technically Correct

It was the fifth time he'd said it; "two eggs over easy and I want them NOW!"

"This 'aint a magic act" I replied, "you'll get 'em when I'm ready!"

I was new to the breakfast grill. It was already incredibly nerve wracking for me, remembering the recipes and styles, keeping up with the incredible speed at which everything takes place when eggs and cakes meet 500 degree steel.

I suppose he was in the right; room service was to get cook's priority. Still, there were two obstructions. One, he was snotty, and I have an aversion to contempt. The second, sad but true, he was male, the house servers were female, and I was incredibly sexist, or chivalrous as I liked to call it.

My patience though finally gave out on his sixth shout. I set a plate on the aluminum shelf between us, and another on the shallow table in front of me. Into the lower I cracked two farm fresh eggs, and then asked the gentleman if he'd said "over easy?" He gave me a sneer before mouthing "about fucking time".

It was then I raised the lower plate over my head, inverting it at the zenith before slamming it down on the shelved plate that he'd already been reaching for.

As pieces of yolky commercial china flew, at least one shard to each of the 360 degrees that make up the "circle of life", I said "Over easy it is sir. Have a lovely day."

Hola Poochito, Como Estas?

It was nearing four AM and whatever drives me to stay awake unto the ruination of my health and livelihood was waning; I was yawning violently, had lost my thirtieth spider solitaire game in sequence and every arthritic bone in my body was shouting "to bed moron, what the hell's wrong with you!" So I powered down and walked to the shack door, waiting until the computer's fan switched off before flicking off the lights. I knew it would be bitterly cold and near pitch black but it's a short walk to the house and the somber light of the moon would be enough to guide me there speedily. With a gasp and a flurry I rushed through the door onto the small wooden platform that serves as my stoop, gingerly closing the glass storm by hand so as to lessen its heavy-weighted clank. And just as my fingers were caught between the door and its frame I noted a shadowed figure a few feet to my right, the frosty smoke of its measured breathing hovering about a head as large as mine, though somewhat more pointed.

We'd caught each other mid thought, and both had blanked out for that moment; both succumbed to the combination of fear, elation, surprise and curiosity, a paralyzing brew of emotion shared by man and beast.

He was bigger than I'd truly thought his kind would be, yet smaller than I'd imagined in wakeful nightmares wherein packs of dogs would chase me through the sedge and lady's thumb and stinging nettle that rises six feet above our boggy back yard. A Lassie sized mutt I figured; fifty to seventy pounds of scrawny, flea bitten howler who at that moment was obviously hungry enough to search the grounds near my own marked scent, risking retribution for trespassing on my turf, hoping to find a jackrabbit or even a mole who'd blindly wandered from his tunnel.

It was frighteningly cold; a few portions of my skin lay bare to the north wind as I hadn't anticipated hesitation much less emulating statuary. Yet it was a moment I didn't want to lose, huffing in time with a wild animal, sharing a space if just for a minute or two admiring each other's power and grace. So I grit my teeth and stood still, as did my challenger, surely more nervous than I and trying to blend into the background more than sate his desire to be at one with nature.

He looked away once, then twice; gauging distance and mapping obstacles, memorizing track and choosing a waypoint. I shushed slowly, then whispered "it's ok, I won't hurt you" through my teeth, as if I knew he was a native coyote and not a recent transplant who only spoke Spanish. But I didn't know Spanish for "nice doggie" anyway, so shhhh was the best I could do.

The cold won the day, the cursed arctic express and its malicious screaming bent us both to searching for shelter and with what I choose to think was a knowing nod, my new friend backed up a step then turned and walked off, never looking over his shoulder. Either he trusted me at that point, or he was wishing I'd just kill him and save him from the rest of what will likely be a horridly cold winter.

Once in the house I had to catch my breath and let my flesh respongify. And as I stood there I thought...I don't have it so bad, I have a house to go to; a heated house and a wife and a dog and plenty of snacks and a computer and aether pals and more stuff than I could carry in a backpack. My hair isn't matted and I don't have to chase bugs to eat and I can catnap without fear of farmers shooting me (well I think I can anyway).

And then I giggled and thought that's all nonsense, there's no relationship between a human and a coyote, he and I have nothing in common. Except the pattern of our breathing, one winter's night under a half lit moon.

Road Song

One hand on the rudder and one on the pen
One eye on the road that I'm pounding again
The radio's chanting I should pull off and shop
But I promised already to drive 'till I drop

Six hundred miles bagged and five thousand to go
How far's not the question, but which way to go
With luck I'll be deep into mountains tonight
Charting stars by the million and roads by their light

And I'll ride the white horse until she sets me down
And I'll search for the place where my roots know the ground
If I pass you don't worry, I'm lost but I'm fine
It's a mad combination, but the madness is mine.

Ron Runeborg

The Last Stop

The train jolted Ania awake. For a moment she was confused and afraid.

"Are we there yet Mama?" she asked as she tugged at her matka's sleeve.

"I believe we are not there yet my darling. Let us hope we are never there and we ride this train forever."

The pair dozed another hour until grinding wheels and tooting whistles signaled a stop in progress.

"Are we there yet mama?"

Krystyna held her little girl close and whispered "Yes dziecina, now do you remember all I told you?"

"Do not speak unless spoken to, do all I am told, be brave. Was that all mama?"

The train ground to a halt. Twenty six boxcar doors slammed open simultaneously reminding the passengers of the artillery shelling their village had absorbed only a week prior. As those aboard were rousted from their rest Krystyna said loudly "and always remember your mother loves you more than life itself. More than LIFE ITSELF!" she shouted as an SS soldier dragged her child from her arms.

"Please step to the ground and form a single line" came a loud cancerous voice from behind a group of snarling dogs. "Welcome to Buchenwald meine kleine Juden."

Johnny on the Spot

"Listen" said the fetus, "I'm not coming out until my demands are met!"

"But you'll kill your mother" God said, "No child of mine would deliberately kill her mother!"

"Well there ya have it grandpa" answered the fetus. "Either I'm taken care of or I grow so big this woman explodes!"

God replied softly, "Alright, what is it you want exactly?"

"I want a guarantee that when I go through this life and then die and I'm reincarnated, I come back as a winged horse!"

"Kinda jumpin' the gun aren't you? Don't you think you might change your mind one day? Besides, life is not about guarantees!"

"Still" the fetus said with a sneer "it is what it is. Now write me that contract!"

"Well child, you have the wrong deity anyway; you want Buddha I'm afraid, but here, I'll connect you."

Somewhere a phone rang. (Atop a mountain most likely)

"Buddha's office, Dalai Lama speaking, is this the angry fetus?"

"It is buster, now fix this problem for me or I swear I'll…"

"I'm terribly sorry, or I would be had I done anything incorrectly or if sorrow wasn't a wasted emotion; you see we're all booked up right now, we're not taking reincarnation reservations at the moment. I can though transfer you to a deity that can straighten out your crooked path if you would be willing to skip this lifetime altogether and jump directly into the winged horse aspect."

"Well… HECK YES! I hate it in this sweaty womb. Let's get the ball rolling! said the fetus.

"Alright madame, I'll transfer you, and thanks for flying Buddha."

Somewhere a phone rang. (Quite near a giant flying eye topped volcano if I'm not mistaken)

"Hello, Johnnygod Tolkein speaking. A winged horse you say? What a delightful proposition…"

And so the Rohan Pegasus was born…

Old Shorts and Poetree

Broken Window's Right Idea

On the planet of Constructor, on the continent of North Barbarica, within the boundaries of the State of Disassembly, in the village of Everfull-Armoire and the neighborhood called Butt Joint populated entirely by the native Barbarican tribe named Wastepipe, four young teens were trying to decide on what to do with their holiday weekend.

"I say we hammer" said Rusty Hinge.

"We just hammered last week!" complained Little Sawhorse. "Besides, you know Swollen Thumbs doesn't hammer anymore!"

"Yea" said Swollen Thumbs, "How 'bout we screw! I've had enough hammering to last a lifetime!"

"I know" said Broken Window excitedly; "let's pretend we're on a planet where everything isn't about tools and crap! Let's pretend we have ray guns and we're trying to save Constructor from a terrible alien infestation!"

"Nah" said Little Sawhorse, "that's silly. My mom says aliens don't exist!"

"Your mom's a Spongemop!" said Rusty; "What does she know?"

On board the spaceship Corporaton, Chairman Evil Doer listened in to the boys' conversation while salivating on his monogrammed shirt and rubbing his hands in glee.

"The fools" Chairman Doer shouted to his General Contractor, "they will offer no resistance! Once we suck this planet dry of its resources, I will be Hardware King of the Universe!"

Another Day in Monsterville

Jerry was new to the area, but not to his trade. With his long resume and charismatic personality he was hired immediately at Happy Harry's House of Furniture. His first day was quiet and uneventful, though a few of his customers were dressed quite garishly and made him more than a bit nervous. "I'd have thought long flowing multicolored crinoline skirts, huge hoop earrings and bandannas had gone out of style" he said to a coworker who smiled grimly in response. His second day was more challenging.

Shortly after punching in, Jerry was standing near the leather collection when the entrance door flew open with a boom and blast of white light. What followed was difficult to fathom. A man, nay a thing approximating a human being shambled through the opening, its arms held upright and forward, dripping a greenish ooze. Jerry stood frozen by fear as the being limped to his side and then turned its head completely around, slowly, while little crackling sounds rifled throughout the building as if all the beast's bones were being broken and then reattached.

"Hello" it finally said. "I'm looking for a nice recliner, which would you recommend for a creature of my stature?' Sadly Jerry was unable to help the new customer. He'd fainted dead away.

Spacin' With Mom

Generally, when my mother's schizophrenia was taking control, she would sit in our kitchen and smoke her brains out while staring out the windows. I was sure my best course of action at those times would be to just disappear; but I never followed up on my rational choices. Even as a kid I thought I could do something about her quandary; I could help her, maybe even save her, and in the process save myself from feeling so incredibly helpless during every minute of every day that I wasn't trying to make the world right.

All I really had in my toolkit was the gift of speech and the ability to tell tales, with which I thought I could divert her attention, move her focus, make clear that she was not alone and that the world was not truly against her.

None of that really affected her. It helped me to be doing something but until I truly understood what her illness brought to her, I was just dancing in quicksand.

And then one day I came home high as a kite on LSD. My mother was up, and in her customary position at 3AM; at the kitchen table, giant glass ashtray overflowing with butts smoked right into their filters, coffee steaming in her cup. Even though I'd pretty much checked out of real life by then, by 15 as it was, I still had some "fear" of my mother discovering my true self; my drug use, my punkishness, my "so unlike the first American Pope I was supposed to be" lifestyle. So, confident in my ability to be stoned out of my mind and still carry on a relatively sentient conversation, I pulled up a chair and added my contributions to the ash pile.

She was in "that place". I knew it by the snappy vitriol aimed at my father, the poor moron that was at that moment outdoors cranking brakes on boxcars in 20 below weather, trying to make enough money to support his people. I argued, but in a calm way; I was far too incapacitated to debate so I kept my comments in the "tepid disavowal" category. Sometimes that turned her wrath onto me, which I thought was fine as men are trained to accept pain as a natural burden. "I can take it" I'd always tell myself as she'd shred my soul with hatred I knew was illusion created by crossed wires.

But this night she seemed almost placid, as if she'd resigned herself to her misery and was simply taking a few last halfhearted gasps at vengeance. And then an odd thing started happening; we both began to cycle in and out of reality in sync.

If you've never tried LSD I can only explain what happens simplistically. It's generally an eight hour "trip", half of which is a build up to a "climax", a short lived hold at maximum high, and then a wafting back to the ground called "spacing out" or probably a hundred other names. People are affected differently of course so much of this is generalization, but it's the "coming down" portion I'm referencing here.

For about 4 hours you drift in and out of the drug's spell; ten minutes feeling perfectly normal but tired and not very energetic, and then you drift away into this other place of your brain's own making. Where "it" is exactly is obviously unique to you, how you perceive it is pretty much the same each time you go; you might be frightened, confused, out of body (ish), angry or euphoric. You might go blind in effect, seeing nothing but swirling colors and elongated trails made by physical movements within your periphery, or you might have absolutely vivid hallucinations of what seem to be real objects or even beings; the old conversation with a unicorn thing.

So, she and I would drift off into our little made up worlds for however long it took for our minds to make their case, and then we'd be back, having a conversation. After a few times on that Ferris wheel it dawned on me that we were on the same carnival ride but in two different circuses. I started to ask her about what she was seeing, what she heard. I asked her in some way I can't recall, but it seemed to make sense to her. She didn't glare at me like I was accusing her of being crazy, and she didn't ask the obvious question "what the fuck are you talking about". She just started talking.

By the end of that experience I was a new man. I had zero academic understanding of mental illness, I couldn't even make what I'd learned a tangible enough thing to describe it to anyone else, not that anyone else was interested in listening to me at that time anyway.

But after years of dealing with this "thing" raising its ugly head from somewhere within my sweet mommy, without even 5 expensive minutes of explanation from the bevy of "professionals" who dealt with her and by association with my siblings and I, after banging my head on random walls throughout my junior high days because I couldn't just FIX the problem even though I'd been told I was gifted and really, really smart and should be able to conquer almost anything I set my focus on... I suddenly "got it". Not the words she heard, not her visions specifically; and yet I'd been to her world, I'd seen those shadows, I'd walked the paths, felt the cold, lost. all. hope; and then gained it back again.

I'd had all those experiences before, far more times than I'd like to admit, but I'd never made the connection.

It was a new day for me. I was actually able to help more, to calm, to reassure, to anticipate, to just plain deal. I'd learned that thing you can't really have until you walk in at least a pair of shoes similar to those the focus of your attentions has been walking in all their lives. I'd learned empathy.

I wrote a poem about the experience. It's said in my voice, and really is about me, at least in the abstract. But it's of the memory of that night, of a scene involving two lost souls wandering through an unknown place, alone, anxious yet fascinated by... by what exactly...

If on the morrow I've been lost, found lacking every social grace please leave me to my rocking, as I'm bound to crawl back home. It's comfort that I'm after, it's a shelter from this maddening pace; it's lessening by a hundred beats, life's taunting metronome

If you've come by and find me mute, give time that I'll relearn my voice. Please sit with me if you've the will, that I might know your care. It's metaphor that I've misplaced, I've not one more grammatic choice to paint the prison I've become, to lay my anguish bare

If this is asking more from you than all you have and then more yet I understand and hold no grudge, I'm comfortable alone. But please don't fear, just walk away and leave me here with no regret…

Once comes my reawakening, I'll tell you all I've known.